THE GODDESS OF DEATH
LA SANTA MUERTE

NYPD OCCULT EXPERT
DETECTIVE MARK MORENO PREPARES
TO FIGHT THE DEVIL'S OWN

MARCOS M. QUINONES, ED.S.

Wasteland Press

Shelbyville, KY USA
www.wastelandpress.net

The Goddess of Death: La Santa Muerte:
NYPD Occult Expert Detective Mark Moreno
Prepares to Fight the Devil's Own
by Marcos M. Quinones, Ed.S.

First Printing – August 2013
ISBN: 978-1-60047-892-5

Printed in the U.S.A.

0   1   2   3   4   5   6   7   8   9   10   11

This Book is Dedicated

to

God Almighty

Jesus Christ

Holy Spirit

1

The Forces of Good versus the Forces of Evil

"40,000 Cops Patrol the City of New York. Only One Patrols the Dark Side."

The only cop that patrols the dark side in the City of New York is NYPD Detective Mark Moreno. He has two doctoral degrees, a master's degree in religion, and a deep desire to serve Jesus Christ through the New York City Police Department. His mission and calling from God Almighty is confronting the Devil, demons, and criminals involved in various forms of the occult. While many may find this line of work frightening, he finds his special mission from God Almighty a lot of fun.

Detective Moreno directly confronts the Devil through criminals working with the occult, demons, and Satan. Satan strategically applies tactics to snare men and women into sin, destruction, devastation, and death. The Devil understands human nature and psychology. The whole world desperately needs salvation through Jesus Christ.

> "...the snare of the devil, having been taken captive
> by him to do his will." 2 Timothy 2:26

> "...the whole world is under the sway of the evil one."
> 1 John 5:19

In his professional and personal life, Detective Moreno understands that the world desperately needs the love of God. Unfortunately, the world entangled itself in the desires of all sorts of temptations and sin. Men and women have not humbled themselves before God Almighty. Detective Moreno witnesses the pain and sorrow of those in dire need of Jesus Christ. God Almighty has never let down the world. 1 John 4:7–8 says, "Beloved, let us love one another, for love is from God, and whoever loves has been born of God and knows God. Anyone who does not love does not know God, because God is love." 1 Peter 5:6–7 says, "Humble yourselves, therefore, under the mighty hand of God so that at the proper time he may exalt you, casting all your anxieties on him, because he cares for you."

The world needs to live in faith of Jesus Christ and not depend on the useless and powerless idols roaming the world. The reason these idols are useless stems from the fact that they cannot save anyone and offer eternal life. They offer the world eternal death and will lead you to eternal damnation.

"But God shows his love for us in that while we were still sinners, Christ died for us." Romans 5:8

"I have been crucified with Christ. It is no longer I who live, but Christ who lives in me. And the life I now live in the flesh I live by faith in the Son of God, who loved me and gave himself for me." Galatians 2:20

"But God, being rich in mercy, because of the great love with which he loved us, even when we were dead in our trespasses, made us alive together with Christ—by grace you have been saved..." Ephesians 2:4–5

Detective Moreno investigates cult and occult cases within the New York City Police Department, with federal, state, and city law enforcement officers, and international law enforcement agencies and governments. He is on twenty-four-hour call and he enjoys getting the 3:00 A.M. calls because he knows the call is serious. From years of experience, he knows calls after midnight involve tremendous violence related to the occult.

He prefers to work alone when conducting an investigation because he trusts no one; he'd rather pay for his own mistakes and not the mistakes of others. He will only work with a male or female Christian partner. If a mistake occurs during an investigation, Satan and his demons gain the upper hand.

Law enforcement requires experience, skill, and a strong stomach and psyche. Cult and occult investigation is the most dangerous game of life and death anyone can become involved with because the game involves the human soul. This is spiritual warfare. Police officers and criminal investigators are not prepared to handle occult criminal cases because of the destructive, demonic connection. Detective Moreno perceives his line of work as the CSI of the occult. You cannot find Satan with a scalpel or magnifying glass—you find Satan, demons, and elements of the occult with the assistance of God Almighty through a relationship with Jesus Christ.

The battlefield for spiritual warfare is the Planet Earth. Spiritual warfare involves Satan and his millions of demons opposing God Almighty, Jesus Christ, and the Holy Spirit and Satan's attempt to destroy and kill mankind. Detective Moreno believes that since the fall of Satan and his demons from grace in heaven, they constantly attempt to destroy and kill mankind because Satan and his demons hate God Almighty, Jesus Christ, and the Holy Spirit immensely.

The Bible composes a logical and chronological sequence of events about Lucifer's creation and fall from grace in heaven. According to the Bible, Satan was originally created by God Almighty as Lucifer – the Enlightened One. He was made perfect with free will by God Almighty, created as the highest-ranking cherub in the angelic world. He ruled over every existing angel. Lucifer was created perfectly by God Almighty in all his ways, but in him, iniquity was found. Lucifer's iniquity was *not* created by God – Lucifer chose self-worship through pride. The Bible does not say how long it took from Lucifer's creation for him to rebel against God, but the betrayal actually occurred.

2

Detective Moreno Notes

In the Bible, Ezekiel 28:12–15 states, "Son of man, take up a lamentation upon the king of Tyrus, and say unto him, Thus saith the Lord GOD; Thou sealest up the sum, full of wisdom, and perfect in beauty." It continues:

"13 Thou hast been in Eden the garden of God; every precious stone was thy covering, the sardius, topaz, and the diamond, the beryl, the onyx, and the jasper, the sapphire, the emerald, and the carbuncle, and gold: the workmanship of thy tabrets and of thy pipes was prepared in thee in the day that thou wast created."

"14 Thou art the anointed cherub that covereth; and I have set thee so: thou wast upon the holy mountain of God; thou hast walked up and down in the midst of the stones of fire."

"Lucifer was not an earthly king, as the word 'cherub' is only used in references to angels. God Almighty created millions of different ranks of angels. They were created to do God's will."

"15 Thou wast perfect in thy ways from the day that thou wast created, till iniquity was found in thee."

Isaiah 14:12–15 says, "How art thou fallen from heaven, O Lucifer, son of the morning! How art thou cut down to the ground, which didst weaken the nations!"

> "[13] For thou hast said in thine heart, I will ascend into heaven, I will exalt my throne above the stars of God: I will sit also upon the mount of the congregation, in the sides of the north."
>
> "[15] Yet thou shalt be brought down to hell, to the sides of the pit."

Since the beginning, Satan wanted to be God Almighty. 2nd Corinthians 4:4 states that Satan has become the "god of this world." I find this story amazing because heaven, being the most perfect realm of existence, had an attempted corporate takeover. In the Bible, Revelation 20:10 tells us that Satan will be eternally punished for it. One third of the millions of angels sided with Satan and became demons at this point. Revelation 12:4–9 says, "And his tail drew the third part of the stars of heaven, and did cast them to the earth…"

The expulsion of Satan and his demons from heaven is found in Revelation 12:7 says, "[7]And war broke out in heaven: Michael and his angels fought with the dragon; and the dragon and his angels fought, [8]but they did not prevail, nor was a place found for them in heaven any longer. [9]So the great dragon was cast out, that serpent of old, called the Devil and Satan, who deceives the whole world; he was cast to the earth, and his angels were cast out with him."

Satan rebelled against the Godhead in Heaven. The doctrine of the Godhead is one of the most important concepts in the Bible as well as one of many Biblical mysteries. The Bible specifically mentions the term "Godhead" representing God Almighty, Jesus Christ, and the Holy Spirit. Scripture teaches that God is one, and that God is three. The Godhead is one God existing in three persons – God the Father, the Son, Jesus Christ, and the Holy Spirit. The Godhead is co-equal, co-eternal, and co-existing in power and glory. Each has a specific role in our lives. God Almighty, Jesus Christ, and the Holy Spirit are divinely equal to each other. Our finite minds cannot fully understand the divine concept of the Godhead. The biblical term "Godhead" (theiotes) occurs three times in Scripture, Act 17:29; Romans 1:20; Colossians 2:9. The word "Trinity" is not found in Scripture.

> "Forasmuch then as we are the offspring of God, we ought not to think that the Godhead is like unto gold, or silver, or stone, graven by art and man's device." Acts 17:29

> "For the invisible things of him from the creation of the world are clearly seen, being understood by the things that are made, even his eternal power and Godhead; so that they are without excuse." Romans 1:20

> "For in him dwelleth all the fullness of the Godhead bodily." Colossians 2:9

Detective Moreno knows that Satan and his demons are responsible for many of the occult crimes committed by groups or individuals. Such crimes include bribery, robbery, burglary, assault, arson, desecration of religious facilities and cemeteries, kidnapping, human slavery, prostitution, rape, drug trafficking, gun trafficking, animal cruelty, animal sacrifice, homicide, and human sacrifice.

Individuals or groups involved in some form of the occult become very arrogant and confrontational against law enforcement authorities and other authorities because these criminals believe that their gods, goddesses, or occult powers will protect them against other criminals, police, or civilians. Law enforcement officers need to understand that these criminals are strengthened by demonic entities known as demons that will physically, psychologically, and spiritually harm or kill law enforcement personnel and society. The reason for this is that this is spiritual warfare at its worse.

The destructive strategies of Satan against mankind reflect his extreme hate for God Almighty, Jesus Christ, and the Holy Spirit. Satan knows that God loves men and women, offering Jesus Christ as an offering for our sins, resurrecting Jesus Christ on the third day, and now He reigns in heaven! Alleluia.

In dealing with hundreds of occult cases, Detective Moreno protects himself against Satan and his demons by his relationship with God Almighty, Jesus Christ, and the Holy Spirit. He wears the armor of God that represents truth, righteousness, the Bible, faith, salvation, prayer, and supplication. God Almighty selected Detective Moreno to investigate occult cases for the New York City Police Department because God reads the human heart. In the eyes of God, Detective Moreno is perfect for this calling.

Since the fall of Satan, he has not let up but continues to deceive and destroy men and women with various tactics and strategies. The world needs to understand that Satan is man's worse enemy. To deny his existence gives Satan more power; to join forces with him assures the wrath of God Almighty.

> "[10] Finally, my brethren, be strong in the Lord and in the power of His might. [11] Put on the whole armor of God, that you may be able to stand against the wiles of the devil. [12] For we do not wrestle against flesh and blood, but against principalities, against powers, against the rulers of the darkness of this age, against spiritual *hosts* of wickedness in the heavenly *places*. [13] Therefore take up the whole armor of God, that you may be able to withstand in the evil day, and having done all, to stand." Ephesians 6:10–13

> "[14] Stand therefore, having girded your waist with truth, having put on the breastplate of righteousness, [15] and having shod your feet with the preparation of the gospel of peace; [16] above all, taking the shield of faith with which you will be able to quench all the

fiery darts of the wicked one. [17] And take the helmet of salvation, and the sword of the Spirit, which is the word of God; [18] praying always with all prayer and supplication in the Spirit…" Ephesians 6:13–18

3

Short History of Detective Moreno

Detective Moreno spends hours at the gym lifting weights and eating a well-balanced diet, and does not drink alcohol nor do drugs. Many people may feel that this style of living is boring, but the body is the temple of God. In the Bible, 1 Corinthians 6:19 states, "Or do you not know that your body is the temple of the Holy Spirit *who is* in you, whom you have from God, and you are not your own?"

Detective Moreno reads the Bible every day for one hour. He practices the teachings of the Bible through his life on a daily basis. He also reads the Bible together with Gabriel and Lynette. Gabriel learns very fast and loves to apply the teachings in his life. He lovingly corrects his friends when they say or do something sinful. Gabe is a strong leader for those around him.

Detective Moreno has a compassionate, gentle, and loving nature. He believes that everyone deserves respect regardless of who they are. He will never allow anyone to physically abuse a suspect. Everyone he arrests receives a small Bible tract to introduce Jesus Christ into their lives. Many prisoners arrested by Detective Moreno accepted Jesus Christ on the spot. This was a wonderful experience. Amen. This is not a policy of the police department, but prisoners need reading material to keep them occupied during the arrest process.

At the age of 15, Detective Moreno fell in love with professional wrestling. He was trained at 19 by WWE professional wrestler names Johnny (the Unpredictable) Rodz. Detective Moreno met him at the

Gladiator Gym located on 1ˢᵗ Street and Avenue B. Johnny Rodz trained Detective Moreno one-on-one for a year in professional wrestling. Detective Moreno learned every hold and move that Johnny Rodz taught him; he believes that every wrestling hold is a submission hold when applied properly.

Detective Moreno wrestled for many local promoters, winning all of his matches. He had a very muscular build and wore a mask similar to the Mexican masked wrestlers. Moreno's favorite wrestlers were WWE World Champion Pedro Morales and Mil Mascaras. Morales and Mascaras were tag-team partners on the West Coast and Morales came to the WWE, which was then known as the WWWF. After years of wrestling, Detective Moreno decided to become a police officer and wrestle Satan and his millions of demons. Satan was already defeated by Jesus Christ for the World Heavyweight Championship!

Detective Moreno practices at the pistol range three times a week. When he can, he shoots 1,000 to 1,500 rounds a week. At his home, Detective Moreno has an arsenal of firearms, including a Smith and Wesson, a Sig, a Ruger, Special Forces assault rifles, sniper rifles, and various caliber ammunitions. He always carries a backup gun and a knife. You will find a can of mace in his pocket when lethal action is not necessary. His favorite backup weapon is the Beretta Bobcat 22 caliber with specially made yellow jacket hollow-point stingers. Small, lethal – you do not want to be shot by this weapon.

His wife Lynette loves him very much. If you asked Detective Moreno, she has great taste. They met when Detective Moreno worked at the New York City Police Academy. She instantly fell in love with him. She thought he was a priest when she first met him – at first glance, she perceived his innocence. When he first saw her from behind, he thought she was from the Philippines, but Lynette is from Trinidad and comes from a family of six sisters and two brothers. Her favorite brother, Pedro, recently died of cancer. Pedro's annoying personality irritated Detective Moreno. Even though Pedro was an annoying person, Detective Moreno misses his annoying personality and his beautiful singing voice.

Detective Moreno remembered the time Pedro and Lynette went to purchase a personal vehicle. The car dealer almost threw Pedro out because Pedro was stepping on the gas pedal of the vehicles to test the motor. He was stubborn and bone-headed, but lovable, just like Lynette. (Ssh, do not tell her Detective Moreno said that.)

To add insult to injury, Pedro convinced Lynette, who then convinced Detective Moreno, to pick out a blue Ford Crown Victoria that was as big as a tank. Thank God, Detective Moreno recently purchased a Chevrolet Impala. The Crown Vic was a very good vehicle previously owned by the Missouri State Troopers.

Lynette gave Detective Moreno the greatest gift of his life – his son Gabriel. Gabriel was born two days before Detective Moreno's birthday. Gabriel was born with long, wavy black hair down to his shoulders. He has a beautiful complexion, like his wife Lynette. As a baby, Gabriel was always busy playing with toys. He is a fast learner and very creative.

Now 14 years old, Gabriel is extremely handsome and loves baseball, music production, acting, and modeling. His greatest love is baseball and hopes to play for the New York Yankees. Detective Moreno loves Gabriel very much and Moreno protects his family to the death. He will go ballistic if anyone attempts to hurt his family. The amount of fury he would unleash at his enemies would make them regret they ever started with his family.

As a Christian, Detective Moreno believes in compassion for all human beings, including criminals who make the wrong choices that lead them to incarceration. Before Christ comes into your life, we are prisoners of our sinful nature and remain in bondage and darkness. The light is Jesus Christ that leads us out of darkness, and he releases us from bondage.

Psalm 41:1–2 says, "Blessed is he who has regard for the weak; the LORD delivers him in times of trouble. The LORD will protect him and preserve his life; he will bless him in the land and not surrender him to the desire of his foes." Psalm 86:15 says, "But you,

O Lord, are a compassionate and gracious God, slow to anger, abounding in love and faithfulness."

Law enforcement officers must be compassionate professionals when dealing with a number of situations in their profession. Policing is a people business. Law enforcement officers wear many hats, depending on the situation. One moment, you are dealing with a lost child, making a death notification, and the next you are dealing with a gun-wielding suspect. These situations occur every single day. If you do not like people, law enforcement is not the profession for you.

Detective Moreno does not allow any fellow law enforcement officer to physically and verbally abuse any civilian or prisoner. Not only is this criminal, but totally wrong. No one deserves to be physically and verbally attacked. Every police department has a small group of abusive and corrupt police officers. The victim of such acts suffers psychological and spiritual pain that cannot be eliminated for the rest of their lives.

"Rejoice with those who rejoice, and weep with those who weep." Romans 12:15

"He who is gracious to a poor man lends to the LORD, And He will repay him for his good deed." Proverbs 19:17

"That there should be no division in the body, but that the members should have the same care for one another. And if one member suffers, all the members suffer with it; if one member is honored, all the members rejoice with it." 1 Corinthians 12:25–26

"Have I not wept for the one whose life is hard? Was not my soul grieved for the needy?" Job 30:25

"To the weak I became weak, that I might win the weak; I have become all things to all men, that I may by all means save some." 1 Corinthians 9:22

"He can deal gently with the ignorant and misguided, since he himself also is beset with weakness…" 1 Peter 3:8

"To sum up, let all be harmonious, sympathetic, brotherly, kindhearted, and humble in spirit…" Hebrews 5:2

When a person becomes a Christian, the Holy Spirit enters the person's life. The fruit of the Holy Spirit becomes part of the personality of the Christian. The Christian becomes a new person and the old person of sin dies. In the Bible, Galatians 5:22 states, "[22] But the fruit of the Spirit is love, joy, peace, patience, kindness, goodness, faithfulness, [23] gentleness, self-control; against such things there is no law. [24] And those who belong to Christ Jesus have crucified the flesh with its passions and desires."

The fruit of the Holy Spirit must be part of the Christian law enforcement officer. Professionally, Detective Moreno believes law enforcement officers should love one another and citizens, possess a peaceful heart to bring peace in situations, be kind and gentle to all (especially the elderly and children), and self-control from physically abusing suspects and prisoners, and from corruption and temptation.

In spring of 2002, Detective Moreno was approached by the Central Intelligence Agency about possibly working for them on special assignment because of his cult and occult expertise. CIA supervisor Richard Stevens approached Detective Moreno during training at 26 Federal Plaza. Detective Moreno was training FBI agents, customs officers, and ATF agents. After the training, he invited Detective Moreno for a cup of coffee across the street.

Detective Moreno suspected that the Broadway Café, where they had coffee, had cameras watching them. Stevens ordered a coffee and

Detective Moreno drank cranberry juice. Stevens sat facing the door. Usually, cops sit facing the door in case a gunman comes through the door to rob the location.

"What are your long term goals?" Stevens asked.

"Keep doing what I am doing," Detective Moreno replied. "My reach is international; a special calling from God."

Chuckling, Stevens said, "You truly believe that what you do is a calling from God?"

Detective Moreno closed his eyes and said, "You had a rough two-year marriage because of your daughter's weak heart. You and your wife struggle for her survival as concerned parents. She almost died last year and she is at New York Presbyterian Hospital."

In amazement, Stevens looked at Detective Moreno with tears in his eyes.

"How did you know?

"Let me tell you something. God Almighty selected me to do this line of work because he read my heart. No one is forced to believe me, even though I hope people did believe me for God's glory. He knew exactly where to place me to do his work. I gladly submitted to him in the name of Jesus Christ. "

Stevens listened intensely. "How did you know?"

"When you become a Christian, the Holy Spirit comes into your body and dwells in you. At this point, the Holy Spirit offers Christians nine gifts called the gifts of the Holy Spirit. These gifts are wisdom, word of knowledge, faith, healings, and miracles, prophesy, discerning of spirits, speaking in tongues, and the interpretation of tongues. While sitting here with you, the Holy Spirit revealed to me your home situation through the word of knowledge from the Holy Spirit."

Stevens began to sob quietly at the table. "What is going to happen to my precious daughter? My wife and I cannot live without her."

Detective Moreno says, "Turn to Jesus Christ, and ask him to come into your life as your lord and savior. Believe, and your daughter will be healed."

Stevens never expected this chance meeting to be so personal. He closed his eyes and prayed, "Jesus Christ, I hope I am doing this correctly, but please come into my life, and heal my daughter, please. I beg you. My heart aches unbearably. Please do it for her."

Detective Moreno looked at Stevens and said, "This is the reason why we met; for the glory of God. Do you have a Bible at home?"

Stevens responded, "No, I do not think so."

Detective Moreno reached into his attaché case, removed a Bible, wrote the present month, day, and year, and handed the Bible to Stevens.

Wiping his tears, Stevens took the Bible, and said, "By the way, we can use you at the agency, and you can keep your NYPD job."

Smiling, Detective Moreno answered, "I thought you would never ask. I accept for the Lord Jesus' glory."

Stevens says, "Absolutely." And they shook hands.

As Detective Moreno left the table, CIA Supervisor Stevens received a call from his wife. Nervously, he answered the phone and said, "Hello."

In tears, his wife Helen said, "A miracle just happened. Suzy's heart began to beat strongly, and the doctors removed the life-sustaining machines. She is breathing on her own. They cannot explain it other than a miracle."

Stevens burst out into tears, saying, "Thank you Jesus, thank you. I am coming over. I love you, Helen. I love you so much."

"I love you, too."

Stevens immediately drove to New York Presbyterian Hospital.

4

Detective Moreno Notes 2

Many people believe the Holy Spirit is energy, force, or light emanating from God. The Bible specifically describes the Holy Spirit as a divine person. The Holy Spirit has a personality as a person that thinks, acts, and feels. He possesses a divine mind equal to God Almighty that perfectly thinks. Apart from divinity, these are all the qualities that we possess as human beings.

The Bible specifically demonstrates the personality of the Holy Spirit. In the Bible, we read that the Holy Spirit has a mind, speaks, teaches, directs, forbids, guides, bears witness, hears, and intercedes. Timothy 4:1 states, "Now the Spirit expressly says that in latter times some will depart from the faith, giving heed to deceiving spirits and doctrines of demons..." Acts 8:29 says, "Then the Spirit said to Philip, 'Go near and overtake this chariot.'"

Teaching and evangelism are the greatest professions in the world. Jesus Christ is the greatest teacher in the world personifying the teachings that he taught in his earthly ministry, and defined in the Bible. Interestingly, Detective Moreno believes that Jesus Christ personifies Judaism. Christianity and Judaism are one and the same religions – the Old Testament announces the coming of Jesus Christ through Mosaic and Abrahamic law, and the New Testament offers Jesus Christ as lord and savior to the world.

God Almighty outpoured the Holy Spirit after Jesus was resurrected to Heaven. Jesus said that the Helper sent by God Almighty is the Holy Spirit. John 14:26 says, "But the Helper, the

Holy Spirit, whom the Father will send in My name, He will teach you all things, and bring to your remembrance all things that I said to you." John 14:16–17 says, "And I will pray the Father, and He will give you another Helper, that He may abide with you forever – the Spirit of truth, whom the world cannot receive, because it neither sees Him nor knows Him; but you know Him, for He dwells with you and will be in you..."

According to the Bible, the Holy Spirit has a mind, knowledge, affection, and will. Only a being with personality can possess such qualities. He intercedes for us, can be grieved, blasphemed, insulted, lied to, and resisted. Interestingly, the only unforgivable sin is the blasphemy of the Holy Spirit. One blasphemes the Holy Spirit by questioning and preventing the work of the Holy Spirit in the world.

> "Now he who searches the hearts knows what the mind of the Spirit *is,* because He makes intercession for the saints according to *the will of* God." Romans 8:27

> "For what man knows the things of a man except the spirit of the man which is in him? Even so no one knows the things of God except the Spirit of God." 1 Corinthians 2:11

> "Now I beg you, brethren, through the Lord Jesus Christ, and through the love of the Spirit, that you strive together with me in prayers to God for me..." Romans 15:30

> "And do not grieve the Holy Spirit of God, by whom you were sealed for the day of redemption." Ephesians 4:30

> "Therefore I say to you, every sin and blasphemy will be forgiven men, but the blasphemy *against* the Spirit

will not be forgiven men. [32] Anyone who speaks a word against the Son of Man, it will be forgiven him; but whoever speaks against the Holy Spirit, it will not be forgiven him, either in this age or in the *age* to come." Matthew 12:31–32

Satan can persuade people to lie to the Holy Spirit. When lying to the Holy Spirit, you lie to God. Acts 5:3 says, "But Peter said, 'Ananias, why has Satan filled your heart to lie to the Holy Spirit and keep back part of the price of the land for yourself?'"

According to 1 Corinthians 12:11, "But the manifestation of the Spirit is given to each one for the profit of all: for to one is given the word of wisdom through the Spirit, to another the word of knowledge through the same Spirit, to another faith by the same Spirit, to another gifts of healings by the same Spirit, to another the working of miracles, to another prophecy, to another discerning of spirits, to another different kinds of tongues, to another the interpretation of tongues. But one and the same Spirit works all these things, distributing to each one individually as He wills."

5

La Santa Muerte Religion

Since the Tower of Babel, religions started throughout the world and continued to spread. There are many religious practices in Latin America, including Santeria, brujeria, voodoo, palo mayombe, spiritualism, and La Santa Muerte. Millions of people practice each of these religions while practicing Roman Catholicism and Christianity. Children learn from their parents and children teach their children.

Many Catholics and Christians will simultaneously practice Santeria, brujeria, palo, etc. They turn to these religions when they feel their prayers are not answered, and need a quick fix to their problems. Most people feel that these religions believe the same thing and that these gods and goddesses are identical to the Christian Biblical God. This is farthest from the truth because this reasoning is false.

The term Santeria means worship of the saints. Santeria worshipers deceive themselves in believing that they can worship African deities by the names of Roman Catholic saints. Roman Catholicism has nothing to do with African demons disguising as Roman Catholic saints. The following are names and a brief description of Santeria deities with their Roman Catholic saints:

Chango – God of fire, thunder, and lightning – St. Barbara

Eleggua – Messenger, Protector of the Home – Holy Child of Atocha

Oggun – God of War – St. Peter

Babalu-Aye – God of Diseases – St. Lazares

Ochosi – God of the Hunt – St. Norbert

Obatala – Owner of Whiteness – Creator of mankind – Lady of Mercy

Yamaya – Goddess of the Ocean – Virgin of Regla

Oya – Goddess of the Cemetery – Virgin of La Candelaria

Oshun – Goddess of the Rivers – Lady of Charity

The religion of La Santa Muerte has taken Mexico, Latin America, and the United States by storm. Millions of practitioners daily devote themselves to her in return for her love and favor. Practitioners range from the poor, middle class, upper class, and criminals. La Santa Muerte does not care if you are a law-abiding citizen or a cutthroat criminal. She does not favor anyone in particular – what she cares about is your devotion to her.

The origin of La Santa Muerte religion is speculative and mysterious. The culture of death is very popular in Mexico. Historically, many Mexicans have been fascinated with death.

People believe that death determines when it is time for someone to move to the next realm of existence and that death is a transitional process. Many believe that La Santa Muerte may be the worship of the Aztec god Mictlantecuhtli and the goddess Micttecacihuatl. Traditionally, worshipers offered human sacrifices to these two deities. Allegedly, these deities ate the dead. They were portrayed as skeletons with the power of death, and worshipers sought the victory of the power of death.

According to practitioners, La Santa Muerte is known by many different names. Various names include La Flaca (Skinny One), La Negrita (The Dark One), La Poderosa (The Powerful One), Santa Niña Blanca (The White Lady), La Niña (The Girl), La Bonita (The Pretty Lady), La Flaquita (The Little Skinny Lady), Señora de las Sombras (Lady of the Shadows), Señora Blanca (White Lady), Señora Negra (Black Lady), and La Niña Santa (Holy Girl).

La Santa Muerte appears as a feminine skeletal figure similar to the Grim Reaper. Statues and pictures depict her holding a globe and scythe. The scythe is an agricultural tool for cutting. For La Santa Muerte, the scythe and globe represents that she has world power and dominion. She wears various robes of different colors depending on the owner of the statue.

She has become very popular in the last century in Mexico City, and hundreds of La Santa Shrines throughout Mexico City. La Santa Muerte altars are found in homes and stores. People come and offer La Santa Muerte cigars, cigarettes, fruits, vegetables, food, and prayers. What is important to La Santa Muerte is that you love her and remain devoted to her. She will severely punish you if you betray her or do not meet her expectations.

6

The Truth about La Santa Muerte

La Santa Muerte is a demon impersonating a goddess for the welfare of humanity. Many worshipers of La Santa Muerte and other religions are offended by this statement. The truth is not to offend. The goal of La Santa Muerte in Mexico and around the world is the destruction of the fabric of society where she is worshiped by various groups and individuals.

In the Bible, the worship of La Santa Muerte and other gods and goddesses is called idol worship. The Bible states that when we were pagans, we worshiped the idols, and these idols led us every which way into destruction. God Almighty recognizes the existence of Satan and millions of demons. Idol worship is an abomination against God Almighty. God is a jealous God that does not want us to worship demons impersonating gods and goddesses.

Unfortunately, millions of people worship demons as gods, goddesses, spirits, guides, or dead relatives. This is demonic deception for your destruction and death. According to the Bible, Romans 1:25 says, "Many people exchange the truth for a lie, and worship and serve the creature rather than the Creator, who is blessed forever! Amen."

When you worship idols, God Almighty will punish you and your children to the third and fourth future generations. Idol worship reflects one's hate for God. God does not want us to participate with demons and serve two gods. 1 Corinthians 10:20–21 says, "You cannot drink of the cup of the Lord and the cup of demons. You cannot partake of the table of the Lord and the table of demons." Satan and demons are not gods, even though people worship them as such.

These words are not to offend anyone, but to offer the truth of salvation through Jesus Christ. God Almighty loves us very much. The greatest proof of his love for us was offering his son Jesus Christ as a sacrifice for our sins. Jesus was honored to be an offering in obedience to God and his love for us. On the third day, God Almighty resurrected Jesus Christ to life, to reign forever as lord and savior. "For God did not send His Son into the world to condemn the world, but that the world through Him might be saved" (John 3:17).

Jesus explicitly stated in John 16:28: "I came forth from the Father and have come into the world. Again, I leave the world and go to the Father." And Exodus 20:2–5 states, "I am the LORD thy God, which have brought thee out of the land of Egypt, out of the house of bondage. Thou shalt have no other gods before me. Thou shalt not make unto thee any graven image, or any likeness of anything that is in heaven above, or that is in the earth beneath, or that is in the water under the earth. Thou shalt not bow down thyself to them, nor serve them: for I the LORD thy God am a jealous God, visiting the iniquity of the fathers upon the children unto the third and fourth generation of them that hate me."

Deuteronomy 18:10–12 mentions the nine most powerful and popular occult practices known today. The nine occult practices are human sacrifice, witchcraft, soothsaying, interpretation of omens, sorcery, casting spells, medium, spiritist, and calling up the dead. These occult practices offend God Almighty because occult practices are empowered by Satan and demons.

For example, if your grandmother becomes involved with the Ouija board when she was a child, you can be oppressed or possessed by that demon years later, up to the third generation. The time frame for the effects of involvement in the occult can be 300 years or three generations. Three hundred years of demonic oppression and possession destroys the lives of hundreds and possibly millions of people. Unfortunately, the secular world does not accept the reality of Satan and demons.

7

Pablo's Conversion to La Santa Muerte

Five years ago, in Mexico City, Raul Cruz, a self-proclaimed La Santa Muerte High Priest, introduced La Santa Muerte to Pablo Cruz when Pablo delivered two pounds of marijuana to the home of Raul. The night before, in a dream, La Santa Muerte told Raul, "Tomorrow you will meet a young man delivering a package to you. Bring him to my altar as a servant." Raul was very happy with the request made by La Santa Muerte.

At 9:00 P.M., Pablo and two bodyguards came to the home of Raul with the two-pound package of marijuana. After Raul placed the package in his wall safe, Raul asked Pablo, "I want to introduce you to the Lady. She eagerly waits for your presence."

"That is fine with me. But I have no offering."

"No need because you are the offering she desires as her servant."

"Wow. What have I done to deserve this honor?" Pablo heard about La Santa Muerte through friends, associates, and relatives, but he was afraid to ask about her. He felt he was not worthy of her love.

"Life has a strange way of manifesting blessings to us when we least expect it," Raul said.

Raul led Pablo to another room in the house. As soon as they entered the room, Pablo noticed thirty chairs lined up in five rows. In front of the chairs stood a six-foot stone statue of La Santa Muerte wearing a white hooded robe. Black, white, and red candles, flowers, incense, cigars, money, fruits, knives, daggers, and other items neatly lined the altar. Pablo felt that La Santa Muerte felt at home in this room.

This room serves as Raul's La Santa Muerte chapel. At this location, worshipers visit La Santa Muerte on Monday, Wednesday, Friday, and the first of every month. They bring offerings to La Santa Muerte in return for her protection and love. Raul is well respected in the community, bringing people to La Santa Muerte and providing marijuana sales to those he trusts.

As he knelt in front of the altar, Pablo instantly fell in love with La Santa Muerte. He closed his eyes as he prayed to her. Even though he did not exactly know what to pray for, Pablo felt the connection with La Santa Muerte. Raul poured holy water on the head of Pablo. As Pablo prayed, he felt the spirit of La Santa Muerte enter his body. He felt aroused by her presence inside of him.

Raul said, "Do you accept her, my child?"

Pablo responded, "With all my heart and soul."

"You will love and obey her as she blesses your life."

"Yes, my godfather. I will never leave her."

When Pablo opened his tearful eyes, La Santa Muerte stood in front of him with her bony hands touching his face. Pablo felt no fear but awe in his heart.

In a demonic, deep voice, La Santa Muerte said, "I accept you as my child and servant. I will provide and protect you from all dangers. Obedience is all I ask." She looked at the ceiling and let out a chilling growl and looked at Pablo.

"I accept, my Lady."

La Santa Muerte slowly returned to her original position at the altar. She returned back to stone. Raul stared in amazement. He could not believe what he saw. He heard from believers in the past that La Santa Muerte physically appeared to those she considered important to her ministry, but Pablo thought that those stories were fables. Raul felt honored he was present when she appeared to Pablo. He wondered why La Santa Muerte never appeared to him in the past. He only felt her presence spiritually.

Raul and Pablo stepped to the back of the altar room to a table on the left. They both sat down and Raul said, "I want to tattoo the face of La Santa Muerte on your left forearm. She will always protect you and be near to you."

"Why is she doing this for me?"

Raul responded, "Sometimes we do not need to know the reasons. It is important that we follow through her commandments and desires. She knows our hearts and what is best for us."

"I want to please her with my whole heart."

"Do it, my son. Do it. The only thing you will ever regret is that you did not know her in the past."

Raul spent two hours tattooing the skeletal face of La Santa Muerte on Pablo's left forearm. The tattoo ritual bounded Pablo and La Santa Muerte. Raul brought Pablo to a bathroom and removed his clothing. Pablo knelt in the bathtub and Raul poured oil, herbs, and spices on his head. Pablo felt empowered as the ointment soaked his body.

On this day, La Santa Muerte acquired another lost soul that sought salvation. Pablo deceived himself into believing that La Santa Muerte could offer him or anyone salvation. Demons are real and La Santa Muerte is a powerful demon deceiving millions away from Jesus Christ and his eternal salvation.

Pablo submitted himself to La Santa Muerte for the hope of power and riches. La Santa Muerte works for Satan as one of his demons. Demons are stationed in different countries to oversee the affairs of that country. Keep in mind that demons are very intelligent and powerful against the weak. Pablo's weakness led him to submit his soul to this powerful demon. How sad.

Millions of people tattoo their bodies in different parts with names, symbols, and pictures. There are military, religious, gang, ethnic, cultural tattoos from all over the world and tattoo parlors in every city in the United States. The person etching the tattoo on your body considers himself an artist. The Bible mentions many issues related to the caring of one's body. In the Book of Leviticus 19:28, we read, "Ye shall not make any cuttings in your flesh for the dead, nor print any marks upon you: I am the LORD." God Almighty does not want us to place any sort of tattoo on our bodies or cut into our flesh.

During the initiation process, many religions cut the flesh of their practitioners as part of their membership. The cutting and marking of the body was a heathen practice for the dead, and God does not want us to imitate them. The cutting of the flesh was a practice of the Priest of Baal and currently the practice of Palo Mayombe. Cutting symbolizes one allowing the so-called god, goddess, or demon to enter the flesh of the person. When Pablo allowed the tattoo of La Santa Muerte on his right forearm, he made allegiance with her.

God Almighty wants us to submit to him as soon as we can. It is the greatest decision anyone can make in their lives. The Devil becomes powerless when we submit to God through Jesus Christ as lord and savior. In the Bible, James 4:7 states, "Submit yourself therefore to God. Resist the Devil, and he will flee from you." Once a person accepts Jesus Christ as their personal lord and savior, the Holy Spirit, God, and Jesus Christ dwell in their body. 1 John 4:4 says, "Little children, you are from God and have overcome them, for he who is in you is greater than he who is in the world."

The one in you is the lord and savior Jesus Christ. The one in the world is the Devil who slanders and accuses you before God. Do not think that Satan dwells in hell. He actually roams the world searching for people to destroy. He is not alone but is assisted by millions of demons. 1 Peter 5:8 says, "Be sober, be vigilant; because your adversary the devil, as a roaring lion, walketh about, seeking whom he may devour." The Devil cannot be in all places at the same time; only God Almighty is omnipresent.

In the course of two months, Pablo initiated his girlfriend Maria, and his drug trafficking partners Octavio, Pepe, Tito, Jose, Memo, Luis, Jesus, Manuel, and his best friend Felix. Pablo and Felix grew up together. When Felix's father left the family, Pablo's family took him in. Pablo loved Felix like a younger brother. They never separated from each other's presence.

As the months went by, Pablo's operation in Mexico City grew stronger, richer, and expanded throughout Mexico, including Acapulco, Guadalajara, Senora, Monterrey, and Ciudad Juárez. In fact, many drug cartels feared Pablo because he was dearly protected by La Santa Muerte. Rumors spread that he killed many of the competition through his black magic. No one dared to double-cross him, and those that did disappeared from Mexico or disappeared altogether. Usually that meant that Pablo would kill all his enemies in the most frightening fashion.

Three weeks later, the phone rang in the home of Raul. He picked the phone up and the caller hung up. Raul became suspicious of the phone call and locked his front door. All of a sudden, the lights in his house went out. Not even the emergency generator turned the lights on. Raul picked up his cell phone but it was not working.

Raul ran to his altar room and locked the door. Candles lit the room and Raul heard a noise in the living room. He became scared and hid behind the statue of La Santa Muerte. He prayed to her for protection. Raul held onto the statue of La Santa Muerte and hid his face on the ground.

The door knob began to slowly turn. Slowly the door opened, and three dark-dressed men entered the room. Raul began to shake on the ground as the three men approached him. Raul felt his heart pounding in his chest. As he opened his eyes, Raul saw the first man's heels of his shoes.

As the first man grabbed Raul from the ground, Raul grabbed a wooden staff and swung at the man, striking him in the jaw and sending him flying to the ground. The second male kicked Raul in the chest, making the wooden staff fly out of his hand. Raul hit the ground hard and the first two men grabbed him, and placed him in the altar circle. Raul looked up to see Pablo standing in front of him.

"What is the meaning of this, Pablo?"

"The meaning is I reign King, not you."

"I just brought you into the religion and now you betray me, you worthless scoundrel?"

"Shut up! You just do not get it."

"No, you shut up."

"What you do not understand is that I am your Padrino, godfather? You have betrayed the sacred trust, blasphemy. What you do not understand, Padrino is that I want your power and spirit. La Santa Muerte selected me to reign with her and you have run your usefulness. There is no room in the throne for you."

Raul cried out, "No. No. Stop this immediately!"

The two men held Raul's arms as Raul stood on his knees. Pablo closed his eyes and began to pray to La Santa Muerte as he removed his weapon from his holster and shot Raul in the head, killing him instantly. Raul dropped to the ground, and all the candles in the room went out. Pablo and his men looked in the direction of the Statue of La Santa Muerte. She screamed out loud in approval.

Felix and Octavio looked at each other in fear. They realized that Pablo adored La Santa Muerte and would sacrifice anyone for her. At this point, Felix and Octavio did not know whether they fear La Santa Muerte more than they fear Pablo. They walk a thin line between life and death in the hands of Pablo; a thin line they do not want to cross.

8

Twelve Severed Heads Found in Field

Jose and Maria Gutierrez had been married for twelve years with two lovely children, Jose, 10, and Anna, 8. Maria was a full-time mother caring for her husband and children. Her husband, Jose, was the center of her life. They met at La Virgin Catholic Church and married two years later.

Jose tended his small cattle farm, providing milk and beef for the local community. He learned his skill from his father Pedro. When his father died, Jose kept the business and tradition going. Jose was not sure if the business would continue because his son Jose wanted to be a lawyer, and his daughter Anna wanted to be a journalist. The elder Jose did not care as long as his children succeed.

"Maria, I am going tomorrow to Sanchez to deliver tow steers to him."

"Ok, amor. Just be careful so early in the morning."

Early Saturday morning, Jose walked two cows to be sold to the Sanchez family. Between a row of trees, Jose noticed a black candle on the grass. As he approached the candle, he screamed in horror at the sight in front of him. Staring at Jose were twelve eyeless male severed heads in three rows. The candle was in the front of the severed heads. Jose ran for his life, screaming and stumbling as he ran. He left his cows behind as he ran home yelling, "Maria! Children! Let's run to the house!"

Anna cried, "What's wrong? What's wrong?"

"In the field, human heads, Dios mio! We need to call the police now." Maria gave him the phone and he nervously dialed the police. As he spoke to the police, he felt a dark evil presence surround him.

The police arrived an hour later, and Jose led them to the crime scene. The police did not really believe Jose. Upon arriving to the crime scene location, Police Officer Pedro Ramirez made the sign of the cross. Police Officer Jose Ortiz stopped short and screamed in horror. Ortiz had a reputation for being gung-ho, but this crime scene traumatized him. He did not know whether to faint, throw up, or both. To his horror, he realized that the third severed head to the right in the first row was his 19-year-old cousin Julio, who was a small-time local marijuana dealer in town. Julio was an only child, and this news would break his mother Delia's heart.

Ramirez said, "This is the Devil, the Devil has arrived! We are doomed. Do not touch anything, or the Devil will avenge himself against us."

Ortiz said nervously, "Look, we cannot walk away, Dios mio. We need to call for help and get Father Torres to bless this area and bless us." Crying, he said, "Julio, who did this to you? Primo, who did this to you?"

Three hours later, the local media broadcasted the incident. *La Prensa* newspaper called the story, "El Diablo Takes Twelve Souls to Hell." The Mexican authorities released no details of the case. The authorities were afraid that those responsible for the murders would seek vengeance. In fact, the Mexican authorities avoided investigating the case because no one wanted to end up the same way.

A couple of days later, Pepe Sanchez visited the home of Jose and Maria. When he arrived, he called out for Jose and Maria, but no one answered. He entered the house from the front door. There is no one in the living room. When Pepe entered the kitchen, he found both Jose and Maria on the floor, lying next to each other. In a bowl, next to their heads, were their severed tongues. Their lips were sewn together with thread. There was a red candle next to their feet.

The red candle represented revenge. Pepe immediately called the police on his cell phone. The murderers had killed Jose and Maria because they had called the police about the twelve severed heads. Ritual groups are not afraid to come after civilians and the police. They believe they are above the law and God Almighty. This group believed that their occult beliefs would protect them against God Almighty and the law. The Bible says, "The fool says in his heart, there is no God."

Pepe stumbled to his knees and cried for his friends. He frantically searched the house for the children. He grabbed a 38 revolver that Jose kept in the kitchen drawer, and ran to the barn, calling their names. He heard noise inside a stall; he pointed the weapon and approached the stall. As he opened the gate, he saw little Jose and Anna holding each other. He grabbed them in his arms, saying, "I have you, come, do not worry. I will take care of you. No one will hurt you."

A week later, funeral services were held at La Virgin Catholic Church. There was a lot of fear throughout the town because of the murders. Pepe, his wife, Jose, and Anna were sitting in the front left row. Father Manuel Cortez performed the funeral ceremony. Pepe stepped up to the pulpit. With tears in his eyes, he said, "I do not know what to say. Jose and Maria were my friends and I loved them. I cannot believe they are dead. My wife Minerva and I never had children. We accept Jose and Anna as our own children, to love them."

He looked at Jose and Anna. "We promise to love you always until we die. We will make it as a family, and I know your father and mother wanted it that way. I know they are watching in heaven, loving you always." Pepe looked down with tears streaming down his cheeks. Crying, Jose and Anna held each other. The unbearable pain in his heart echoed through the church. He looked at the cross hanging at the altar, and prayed in silence.

As Pepe prayed, all of the doors of the church closed tightly, and fear permeated the church. A loud roar surrounded the outside church perimeter for ten seconds and then – silence. Many hid underneath their benches, holding each other. People looked around expecting someone or something to come in. To their horror, a black shadow came through the door. An elderly man in the back of the church in a wheelchair stood up and ran to the front of the church. Waving her hand, his wife called to him, "Ito, come! Ito, come!" The shadow flew over the congregation and disappeared over their heads. Father Cortez, who hid inside the pulpit, came out, saying, "God bless everyone. Go in peace," and he ran to the back room of the church.

9

Gabriel and Detective Moreno

At the office of Detective Moreno, located at 1 Police Plaza, he and his son Gabriel sat and talked. They planned to buy baseball equipment at Modell's because baseball season began the next week. Gabriel had a list of baseball equipment worth $300; Detective Moreno would use his excellent reasoning approach to purchase only $125 worth of equipment. Gabriel could be persuasive like a lawyer, convincing anyone his point of view.

"Hey, dad?"

"Yessssss."

"Promise me something."

"What, my man?"

"Promise me you will never die and get hurt. My heart would be in so much pain; I could not function."

"I promise."

"I cannot live without you. Jesus Christ, God, and the Holy Spirit come first. You come next, Dad."

"Amen, my son."

"I promise that I will be with you for a very long time. Besides, I want to play with your kids with all their toys. Also, I want to see you play with the New York Yankees. I will be so proud to see you in your pin strips. Besides, I want to spend a little of your money on nooks and cranny."

Gabriel laughed and hugged his dad.

They headed to Modell's Sporting on Broadway and Chambers Street. Again, Gabriel grabbed the most expensive equipment and argued like a lawyer on how the equipment will make him a better ballplayer. They spent over an hour at Modell's. Detective Moreno bought himself a couple of workout shirts. He spent $165 on Gabriel's equipment.

At the cashier's line, Detective Moreno stared at Gabriel and thought, "What a good boy with such a big heart. I would torture and kill anyone that would hurt you, my son. I am the one that cannot live without you. I know that this is not the way to think as a Christian, but I would be devastated. I pray to Jesus Christ that he blesses and protects you forever."

10

The Ambush in Guadalajara

At 11:30 P.M., Cecil Lopez led his five goats through the grassy cliff. He lived with his young wife Maribel, and his twin 6-year-old daughters, Maria and Susana. The cool breeze swayed the grass back and forth. Cecil took this route every morning, but today he felt uneasiness. Suddenly, his five goats turned around, not wanting to go farther over the left turn on the road. He pulled them by the horns to go forward, but they refused. Cecil turned the bend to observe the shock of his life!

Twenty-five yards in front of Cecil were five men dressed in black cloaks standing inside a white circle. One of the men appeared to be talking to the group with his back to them. One man held a black goat as the leader of the group pulled a dagger. Frightened by the scene, Cecil ran to his home and left his goats behind. He told Maribel to lock the doors and stay home with his daughters. Maribel called their daughters and hid in the bedroom. He called the police; Police Officers Tomas Gutierrez and Juan Gomez came over ten minutes later. Cecil described what he had observed and returned to the scene with the two police officers.

They find an empty white circle and blood on the ground. Gomez bent down and touched the blood with his fingers. As he stood, an arrow struck him in the chest, and he dropped to the ground, dead. Gutierrez yelled, "Oh my God!" He pulled his revolver and radioed, "Centro, we are under attack! I need help! Ayudame!" He heard noise in front of him and fired several shots with his weapon. As he reloaded, a black-hooded male kicked the gun out of his hand. Gutierrez tackled the male and punched him in the face. Another hooded male came from behind and placed a choke-hold around Gutierrez's neck. As they struggled on the ground, Gutierrez flipped the male, punching him several times in the face, knocking the male out. Another male comes from behind and knocks Gutierrez out with his own weapon.

When Gutierrez woke up, drowsy, he was lying on his back on the ground inside of the white circle. At his right was the body of Gomez with the arrow removed. At his left side was the body of Cecil, his throat slit. He noticed two black candles, one on the right of Cecil, and another candle to the left of Gomez. A rotting odor surrounded the area. Gutierrez struggled to free himself, but to no avail.

A black figure holding a dagger in his right hand approached the circle. The red-cloaked male said, "What did you expect to find, to solve?"

Gutierrez said, "Who are you? Turn me loose. Do you know who I am?"

"Shut up!"

A group of men stood around the circle with their heads bowed.

The red-cloaked male said, "I pray to you, my Lady, and offer these three to you this day. Your servant did not expect such offerings to occur, but who am I to know? Accept these offerings as an offering of authority, my Lady." He lifted the dagger as the moon shone upon the blade. The dagger struck Gutierrez' body several times, and the dagger turned red with blood. Gutierrez screamed in excruciating agony.

As Gutierrez opened his eyes, a hideous female skeletal figure stood above him. The huge red eyes stared at Gutierrez and growled as its face moved closer. La Santa Muerte lifted Gutierrez by the neck with one hand. All the men surrounding the circle knelt in fear and awe. One of the men fainted on the ground. The other men trembled as they knelt with their eyes closed. Many of them wondered if this was worth the trouble. Never did they ever expect to experience such terror. All they desired was fame, money, and riches. Proverbs 14:12 says, "There is a way *that seems* right to a man, But its end *is* the way of death"…and La Santa Muerte will lead to death those that worship her.

Suddenly, gunshots struck the circle from ten yards away. La Santa Muerte growled, slammed Gutierrez to the ground, and ran in the direction of the gunshots. The men stood up, pulling their weapons and surrounding the red-cloaked male. In the distance, there were loud growls, gunshots, and screams.

Four police officers stood by their police vehicles. As La Santa Muerte approached them, Sergeant Cortez yelled, "Fire!" Bullets struck La Santa Muerte without causing her harm. The police officers kept reloading their weapons. As La Santa Muerte stepped forward, she grabbed Sergeant Cortez and snapped his neck, killing him instantly. Police Officer Ramirez charged La Santa Muerte and she kicked him in the chest, sending him flying into one of the police vehicles, snapping his back.

La Santa Muerte approached Police Officers Sanchez and Gonzalez. Her presence immobilized them. They screamed in terror as La Santa Muerte grabbed them by the faces and snapped their necks. A Christian crucifix from the neck of Sanchez fell to the ground. When La Santa Muerte observed the crucifix, she yelled a painful growl, dropped the bodies, and jumped back several feet.

Evil cannot stand in the presence of good. The crucifix symbol represents the death and resurrection of Jesus Christ. The cross does not have magical or protective powers. Evil cannot comprehend the significance of the redeeming power of the death and resurrection of Jesus Christ.

Satan and his demons rejected the love of Christ. It was not their nature to ask for forgiveness. Once they made their decision, there was no coming back. Satan and his fallen angels were part of God's heavenly kingdom. They were part of the heavenly realm.

La Santa Muerte growled in the night. Nervously, the men waited for minutes that seemed like hours. She vanished from where she stood. A strong sulphur smell surrounded the area. In many occult investigations, witnesses report the smell of sulphur at the crime scene. Sulphur is associated with hell and demons.

The men trembled as a tall figure entered the circle. The figure held two human heads in each clawed hand and dropped the four severed heads into the circle. The men fearfully stared at the severed heads, as La Santa Muerte screamed in the night. A few minutes later, La Santa Muerte vanished from the circle.

They stood up and stepped away from the circle. The bodies and the severed heads were left inside of the circle. This was considered sacred ground; nothing would be disturbed. The men walked to their vehicles. The red-cloaked male said, "Learn and live. What you have witnessed occurred because of who we are and what we will accomplish. I demand obedience; betrayal will not be tolerated and the result will be death!"

Pablo is a "deceiver and an antichrist" because he is leading his people into destruction and hell. La Santa Muerte rules the soul of Pablo. 1 John 2:18 says, "Little children, it is the last hour; and as you have heard that the Antichrist is coming, even now many antichrists have come, by which we know that it is the last hour." 2 John 1:7 says, "For many deceivers have gone out into the world who do not confess Jesus Christ *as* coming in the flesh. This is a deceiver and an antichrist." Unfortunately, many fall victim to the so-called saviors of the world. Pablo is an antichrist because of his demonic spirit.

As they approached their vehicles, Manuel approached Pablo.

"Hey, boss, I need to speak to you."

Pablo sniffed the air and said, "What do you want? I smell fear."

"Boss, I cannot do this anymore. This is not for me. I know you took the time to initiate me into this religion, but I just cannot continue."

Pablo angrily said, "You're kidding me, right? You just want me to let you walk away, and live a normal life happily ever after?"

Sarcastically, Manuel said, "That's right; I want to live a normal happy life. Get the hell out of my face!"

Manuel shoved Pablo away from him, and Pablo threw a punch at Manuel. Manuel blocked the punch and countered with a right hook that sent Pablo to the ground. In a rage, Pablo stood up, pulled a dagger from his waist, and stabbed Manuel in the heart, instantly killing him. He cleaned the blood off the dagger with Manuel's pants, and placed the dagger back in his waistband.

Pablo never expected anyone to leave or attack him. As Pablo looked at Manuel on the ground, he noticed a crucifix on the neck of Manuel. Pablo considered Christianity an enemy of La Santa Muerte. Pablo realized that the man from Galilee, the so-called Savior of the world Jesus Christ, had touched Manuel.

In the city of New York, Pablo hoped to turn many away from Christianity. He hoped La Santa Muerte would proclaim New York as her city. She would challenge all contenders to the throne, one that will shed blood, pain, and death for her enemies.

No one, including Satan and demons, can totally control men and woman. Satan and his demons are not omnipotent (all-powerful), omniscient (all-knowing), or omnipresent (all-present). These three qualities will make them gods. The only three divine persons united as one that has these three qualities is God, Jesus Christ, and the Holy Spirit.

Men and women need courage, strength, dependence, and trust in Jesus Christ. Psalms 27:14 states, "Wait on the Lord: be of good courage, and he shall strength thine heart: wait, I say, on the Lord. We should trust in the Lord and no one else." Proverbs 3:5 states, "Trust in the Lord with all thine heart and lean not unto thine own understanding." Unfortunately, Pablo depends on his selfish heart and the power of La Santa Muerte that will lead him to eternal death.

11

American Male Sacrificed in Ciudad Juárez

Pablo and his men worked for the Sanchez cartel in Juárez. They ran errands and transactions for two years until Pablo decided to break loose on his own. Jose Sanchez and his brother Pepe did not appreciate Pablo's departure, but they feared Pablo and his black magic. Pablo was their spiritual consultant when La Santa Muerte communicated to Pablo about what Jose should do within his operation. Pablo knew the information was to help Pablo and his men, and not Jose.

In a dream, Pablo bowed down in obedience and pledged to La Santa Muerte, "I will obey and dedicate my operation to your precious name, mi madre." He viewed New York with La Santa Muerte above the city sky. Now he was ready to proceed and succeed, taking on all contenders and competitors.

Pablo hoped that one day he would expand his operation into the United States. One day, he prayed to La Santa Muerte. That night, in a dream, she stood by Pablo in a high mountain and said to Pablo, "I bless you to cross into the United States and establish yourself and your operation in New York. I will protect you against the competition and the authorities. All I ask is for you and your men to be totally dedicated to me, and I will not tolerate disobedience. The penalty is death. Pablo, before you go, I want you to sacrifice a white male from the United States in my name. In front of my altar, you will bring him and I will take his soul. You must do this as soon as possible or else I will remove my blessing from you."

Jumping out of bed, Pablo woke up in a cold sweat, realizing that the dream was a revelation. He held the La Santa Muerte medallion around his neck and kissed the medallion, crying. His tears of gladness assured him that he had made the right decision in worshipping La Santa Muerte and that she loved him very much.

Immediately, Pablo called a meeting at his home. The group sensed Pablo was tense and nervous as he addressed his group. "We have a mission that will take us to new heights. We are expanding to New York City. I am going to focus on opening a club in the Midtown area called La Gloria Club, dedicated to our Lady. The rich and famous will enter through the doors, but all are welcome to come. We will route our product through hand-selected contacts. I will contact my uncle Victor Perez, who is a lawyer, and he will draw up all legal documents and permits. We will honor La Negra with our success and profits."

At that moment, a dark, eerie cloud covered New York City for an hour.

Pablo earnestly felt he had proven himself in Mexico, and understood the marijuana and cocaine demand in the United States. He believed he could be as powerful as La Santa Muerte as her incarnate son. The force in his life was his love for La Santa Muerte and Pablo loved her more than family. Pablo did not realize that he served a demon in La Santa Muerte.

On Friday evening, Pablo knelt down in front of his altar facing the La Santa Muerte statue and prayed, "Santisima Santa Muerte, I beg of you to shine on your servant, and open a path for me in the United States to bring you honor and glory. I ask your permission to open my operation in the states. Others have tried and failed, but I know with you on my side I will succeed beyond my expectation. I ask in your name." This was the first time that Pablo operated from his comfort zone – he knew that he must make things perfect to please La Santa Muerte.

He gave his people precise instructions about victim selection: Pablo believed La Santa Muerte selected a white male to claim his soul representing the United States.

On Saturday evening, Mexico City is booming with tourists visiting the bars, clubs, and resorts. After walking through many of these establishments, Pablo's people decided to enter the Camino Central Resort, and scanned the bar area for their prey. The bar is filled with American tourists drinking, talking, and eating.

Mark Rogers, age 21, is at the bar having a margarita. He's doing his internship for Alliance Global Capital Group in Dallas, Texas, and is in Mexico City to attend his company's job fair. Mark grew up in Dallas with his parents, Mark and Susan, and his brother, Richard. As a Remington College senior, Mark hoped to line up a position at the Alliance Group. He wanted to marry his high-school sweetheart Marie. Being old-fashioned, she could not attend the Mexico trip because her parents would not allow it.

A beautiful, dark-haired female sat next to Mark on his left. She ordered a beer and smiled at Mark. She said, "Hi. What brings you to this resort?"

"Business and school. What about you?"

"Well, I am here with my co-workers."

"I can relate to that."

Mark and Maria spoke for two hours at the bar – to Mark, it felt like only a few minutes. He excused himself to go to the restroom. Maria then slipped a white powder into his drink, stirring it vigorously. Mark returned a few minutes later and finished his drink. Within minutes, Mark became dizzy in his seat. Maria made a quick call on her cell phone, and she grabbed Mark by the arm, leading him out of the bar.

A black SUV parked in front of the resort opened its back door and Maria escorted Mark into the back seat, and he promptly fell asleep. Octavio drove the SUV for forty minutes northeast of Mexico City. Pulling off the road, he drove 300 feet to a shack. In front of the shack, two armed men are standing post. The moon is full and unusually blood-red.

Blindfolded, Mark is escorted into the shack, the interior of which was lit by fifty candles. Illuminated was a white circle on the floor and an altar containing a six-foot stone statue of La Santa Muerte. She wore a red caped robe; flowers surrounded her to the left and right. Her arms were at her sides. A bowl of red and yellow apples, and numerous human skulls facing straight ahead, lay at her feet.

In front of the altar was a small table draped in a black cloth, and a bowl of burning incense. A black candle was placed on each corner of the table and a four-foot sword, knife, and dagger lay side by side. An empty clay bowl rested on top of a black hardcover book. No one is allowed to read or write in the black book – only Pablo. The black book is called the Book of Shadows.

Practitioners of the occult keep a diary known as the Book of Shadows. Satanists and witches keep a Book of Shadows that may be passed on to relatives, friends, and coven members upon their retirement or death. Many practitioners prefer to be buried with it. A Book of Shadows contains information pertaining to religious texts, recipes, prayers, instruction, spells, day-to-day activities, or any information important to the owner.

Mark awoke on a cold cement floor with a massive headache. His arms and legs were tied, and a black hood was placed over his head. He heard shoveling around him, and smelled the odors in the shack. Frightened out of his mind, Mark yelled, "Hello! Is anyone there? Help me. Please, please help me! Let me go!"

Through a door behind the altar, five black-hooded individuals entered the room and stood inside the white circle. Three of the individuals hummed as the other two whispered in prayer. Mark attempted to listen to what they said but couldn't understand them. One individual sprinkled Mark with holy water.

A red-hooded, gowned individual entered the room. There was total silence. The red-hooded male picked up the sword from the altar, walked over to Mark, and placed the sword blade on top of Mark's head. The male facing the statue said, "We are gathered on your behalf, my Lady, to bring you honor, sacrifice, and worship. We pray you accept this sacrifice in return for your blessings as we journey into the United States, spreading your blessings and knowledge to those willing to accept you."

Thunder roared through the sky, and suddenly the earth began to shake. The stone statue came to life, and La Santa Muerte roared as she slowly walked towards Mark. Everyone in the shack dropped to their knees. La Santa Muerte took the sword from Pablo's hand; she cut Mark in the chest. Mark yelled in pain as he fell to the ground. La Santa Muerte grabbed Mark by his head and picked him up.

La Santa Muerte removed the hood from Mark's head, dropping it to the ground. As soon as Mark saw La Santa Muerte, he screamed in horror, staring into her eyeless sockets and skeletal face. She grabbed him by the throat, lifting him from the ground, and squeezed his neck until Mark was dead. Dropping him to the ground, La Santa Muerte struck Mark's chest with her right hand. She removed his heart from his chest and placed it in the clay bowl on the altar.

La Santa Muerte stood in front of Pablo, saying in a demonic growl, "I accept your offering, my servant. His spirit resides in hell. No one can resist my power and dominion – no one. You will never betray me, and if you do, I will cause your loved ones unbearable pain and anguish. Death will be a blessing to them. Obedience and subservience is what I seek from my servants. No other gods will stand before me, especially the man from Galilee."

She kissed Pablo on his forehead and returned to her original position at the altar. Her body turned back to stone; a black smoke filled the floor of the shack, covering Mark's body. Two minutes later, the smoke recedes, revealing Mark's skeleton. The occupants of the shack stood, shocked at the scanty skeletal remains inside the circle. In fear, Pepe began to shake uncontrollably. Pablo grabbed him by the arm. "Be still, my brother. No need for fear to run through your heart. Today we celebrate our victory and right to passage."

Pedro signaled Pepe and Octavio to remove and bury Mark's body in a grave that had been dug earlier. As the men moved the body outside, Pepe was still shaking uncontrollably.

"My man, do not worry," whispered Octavio.

"I am not worried!" Pepe snapped.

"Why are you shaking, then?"

"Hombre, what if we are wrong? I just do not know. Something does not feel right."

"Listen to me, Pepe. There is no turning back now. We have crossed the line of good and evil. We are beyond that. Pablo has our best interest. He will not lead us into shark-infested waters. La Santa Muerte loves us. We belong to her. Do you understand?"

"Yeah, I think I do."

"Ok!"

Pepe regretted that he became involved with La Santa Muerte and Pablo. He'd had recurring nightmares since he dedicated himself to the cause. Never did he ever expect a demon to materialize and own his soul. He wanted out in the quickest way possible. The rest of the team was die-hard worshipers dedicated to Pablo and La Santa Muerte. Pablo breathed, ate, and slept La Santa Muerte; Pablo is one of her minions of death.

Pepe closed his teary eyes and prayed in silence to no one in particular: "What have I done? Is there a way out of this? I need peace and tranquility in my life without this dark cloud looming over me. This is not right, mi Dios. This is not right. I have a bad feeling about all of this."

Octavio and Pepe placed Mark's body in the grave and covered it up. Pepe, noticing a crucifix belonging to Mark on the ground, picked it up and placed it in his pocket. He returned to the shack.

Pablo stared at him and moved away from Pepe when he approached. For some reason unknown to Pablo, he is repulsed by Pepe's presence.

12

Vampire Drug Dealer Sacrificed

At 11:00 P.M., Pablo called a meeting at his New York City club with his people. They sat and ate breakfast, planning the course for the busy upcoming weekend's festivities. Pablo tapped his glass to get everyone's attention.

"Good morning. This will be a hot weekend, so I want everything in order. Tito, Jose, and I are driving to Atlantic City to meet with some people about expanding our traffic route into New Jersey."

"Can they be trusted?" Octavio asked.

"Yes. Basilio from 145th Street and Broadway highly recommended them."

"Cool."

"Cool, so I will see you guys on Sunday. Keep in touch if any problems arise."

At 8:00 P.M., the La Niña Club and Restaurant was packed with beautiful women, men, music, and dancing. Money flew across the bar; everyone was having a wonderful time. The rich clientele spent hours socializing in the club all night long.

Pablo had left Felix in charge this weekend. At the bar, Felix noticed a male dressed in a black suit slip another male a glassine envelope in exchange for money. Pablo allowed no one outside of his own people to deal drugs at the club. This was his territory and domain.

Felix signaled Octavio over and they both approached the male at the bar.

"Excuse me, sir," Felix said, "can I speak to you?"

"Yeah, man. What do you want?"

"Step to the side of the bar, please. What is your name?"

"My name is Vlad."

Smiling, Felix said, "Vlad, you and your people have to leave the club because I saw you dealing drugs."

Two men dressed in black appeared next to Vlad, who bared his fangs in his mouth.

"I am not leaving and neither are my people. So take your taco-ass away from my face," he said and shoved Felix. Felix grabbed and twisted Vlad's right arm, sending Vlad to the ground. Vlad stood to punch Felix, who blocked it and countered with a kick to Vlad's stomach. Vlad's men charged Felix, but they were grabbed by Felix's men before anything could happen. Vlad pulled a knife from his pocket and Felix pulled his gun. Vlad dropped the knife and was escorted out of the club, along with his entourage.

Vlad looked at Felix and said, "This is not over."

Felix said, "Listen, Bela Lugosi, get your bat-ass out of here before I put a spike in your heart."

Vlad and his men leave west on 37th Street.

Felix called Pablo to tell him of the night's events.

"Good work, Felix. Be careful with these creatures of the night. They are revengeful and work in packs."

"Ok, my brother. I will. Good night."

* * *

In the middle of the night, Pablo woke up screaming. His men ran into the room.

Weapon drawn, Tito says, "What's wrong, boss?"

"Let's head back to New York City – now!"

* * *

At 4:30 A.M., Felix walked to his car in the indoor garage. He looked around as he opened the driver's side door when, out of nowhere, Vlad struck him over the head with something blunt. He and his men shoved Felix into a van and drove out of the garage.

The next morning, no one can find Felix. Octavio, Jesus, and Luis checked the garage to find Felix's car still parked. They checked the inside of the vehicle, but found nothing until Octavio noticed a business card on the ground. The business card listed The Vamp Shop, 230 West 19th Street, New York, New York.

"Dios mio," said Octavio.

A car squealed into the garage, heading toward Octavio, who quickly drew his weapon. Pablo rose from the car; wordlessly, Octavio handed him the business card. Pablo fell to the ground in tears and punched Felix's car several times.

"I want these people dead!" he screamed. "You hear me? Dead!"

*   *   *

Located at 19th Street between 5th and 6th Avenues, the Vamp Shop offered the latest vampire paraphernalia, from replaceable fangs to dark clothing and jewelry. It's owned and managed by Richard Cole, known in the vampire world as Vlad. He had shops in New Jersey, Pennsylvania, and Miami. He wanted to expand to the west coast early next year, and begin a vampire church.

He employed five workers that were part of his clan: Casper, Chaos, Damien, Hades, and his girlfriend, Mary. These were designated vampire names given to them by Vlad after he initiated them. Vlad, a full-time vampire, dressed in black clothing, had black hair and eyelids, black nail polish, and permanent fangs. His people were dedicated to him and referred to Vlad as their "Sire." Vlad had initiated them to his clan by a bloodletting ritual. He had made an incision on their left wrists and he had sucked their blood, promising them eternal life.

Vlad believed in the mystical power of blood. Blood is the life of the body. He believed he would live forever as long as he drank human blood. Vlad's charisma stemmed from his psychic power that many vampires possess. A psychic vampire is a person or demon who feeds off the "life force" of other living creatures. They can physically drain you of energy and even kill you. All they have to do is focus on you and your energy is absorbed by the vampire. If you are perceptive enough, you can sense them when they enter the room.

Christians with the "discernment of spirit" gift of the Holy Spirit can recognize the true nature of a person. There are nine gifts of the Holy Spirit given to Christians after they accept

Jesus Christ as their lord and savior.

> According to 1 Corinthians 12:7–11, "But the manifestation of the Spirit is given to each one for the profit of all: for to one is given the word of wisdom through the Spirit, to another the word of knowledge through the same Spirit, to another faith by the same Spirit, to another gifts of healings by the same Spirit, to another the working of miracles, to another prophecy, to another discerning of spirits, to another different kinds of tongues, to another the interpretation of tongues. But one and the same Spirit works all these things, distributing to each one individually as He wills."

These nine gifts are given by the Holy Spirit. Discerning of spirits is the supernatural ability given by the Holy Spirit to perceive the source of a spiritual manifestation and determine whether it is of God, of the devil, of the world, or of man. A Christian can ask for each of these gifts because they are gifts to be used to uplift or edify the Church of Christ. In the Bible, Acts 16:16–18, a girl had psychic powers of fortune-telling that made her the owner a lot of money. The Apostle Paul became aware of the demon inside of her through the Holy Spirit and Paul exorcised the demon out of the young girl.

At the left wall of the Vamp Shop was a bookshelf that led to the basement, where there was an open area for ritual purposes. For a rental price or a jar of human blood, any one or group could rent the basement to perform rituals and ceremonies. Satanists, witches, Santeros, voodoo high priests and priestesses, sorcerers, fortune-tellers, spiritists, and other occult practitioners used the facility. Vlad didn't care what they did in the basement as long as it didn't bring the police to the location. He literally wanted them to clean after themselves. Vlad had noticed one less person come out of the basement on several occasions. Vlad does not ask, and they do not tell.

There were two occasions where Vlad had sacrificed two individuals to his god. One individual was a burglar who stole $5,000 from the wall safe. The burglar had dropped his wallet inside the Vamp Shop and the incident was not reported to the police department. Late one evening, Vlad had sent his men to kidnap the burglar and bring him back to the Vamp Shop. After Vlad cut his throat, they brought his body to the Stevens Funeral Home in Union, New Jersey. One of Vlad's contacts had a crematory oven. The burglar was turned to white dust.

On Friday, at 11:15 P.M., a male entered the Vamp Shop and walked to the left bookshelf. A minute later, two other males came into the Vamp Shop. A male with a black, hooded jacket then entered the store. He approached Vlad. "Hi, I want to rent the basement for the evening. My name's George; can I see the facility?"

Vlad motioned him to the bookshelf that led to the basement. Two other men and a woman entered the store as Mary attempted to close the door. She returned to the register, feeling uneasy about this group of people in the shop.

As Vlad led the man down the stairs, Pablo revealed himself and unleashed a forward kick to Vlad's back, sending him to the bottom of the basement. When Vlad's people heard the commotion, Pablo's men sprang into action.

Mary pulled a dagger from the counter and started swinging it at Maria, who blocked Mary's arm and punched her twice in the face, knocking her out. Chaos leapt at Tito, who flipped Chaos over his shoulder. Chaos quickly stood up and punched Tito in the face. Tito returned two punches and a kick to the stomach. Chaos fell; his fangs suddenly appeared in his mouth. He leapt up at Tito and attempted to bite his neck. Tito pulled out his Glock and fired two shots at Chaos's stomach. Chaos dropped dead on the floor.

Maria shot Damien and Hades both in the chest, killing them instantly.

Three-hundred-pound Casper tackled Octavio and tried to choke him as well. Pepe leapt onto Casper's back, and Casper rammed Pepe into the wall, crushing him. Casper then lifted Pepe by the neck; Octavio ran over and quickly shot two bullets into Casper's head.

"I had him, I had him!" Pepe shouted angrily.

"No, no," Octavio said. "He had you."

Pepe gave Octavio a dirty look that made Octavio laugh as he put up the "Closed" sign on the door. Everyone headed to the basement.

Vlad was prone on the basement floor, his hands and feet tied. Pablo stood above Vlad and said, "You S.O.B., you will regret forever stepping into my club and hurting my brother Felix. I know that you killed him. You think you are evil? I will demonstrate terror to you, terror you never thought existed. Pain will have a new meaning – you will become pain."

Octavio found a jar of human blood inside Vlad's office and handed it to Pablo. Pablo poured a circle around Vlad with the blood. Crying and pleading, Vlad prayed to the beast inside him to come out and protect him. Suddenly, Vlad began to transform into a beast with large red eyes, clawed hands, and large fangs. The beast growled at those around him and lunged at La Santa Muerte.

Pablo and his men kneeled and prayed for La Santa Muerte to appear. La Santa Muerte appeared through the basement wall. The beast leapt at La Santa Muerte and she grabbed it by the throat, slamming him on the floor several times. The beast screamed in pain and clawed La Santa Muerte's face. La Santa Muerte growled in pain. The beast punched La Santa Muerte four times in the face, and La Santa Muerte kicked him back into the circle of blood.

Pablo and his men pulled their weapons and fired at the beast. Bullets entered his body until he dropped to the ground. La Santa Muerte entered the circle of blood with a wooden spike in her hand. Suddenly, La Santa Muerte said in a deep voice, "Pablo, my child, come here," and handed him the spike. Pablo stood over Vlad and said, "This is for Felix, you S.O.B. I am sending you back to hell." Pablo drove the wooden spike into the chest of Vlad, who died instantly.

La Santa Muerte slowly turned around and vanished through the wall. Pablo and his men brought the bodies into the circle of blood. They poured gasoline on them and Pablo lit the match, tossing it on the bodies as they walked out of the Vamp Shop. Pablo entered his car and his people drove off. Within five minutes, smoke began to seep through the front door.

The FDNY broke down the door of the Vamp Shop and ran down to the basement. To their horror, they found the half-cooked bodies. They notified the NYPD and within minutes, detectives from the 13th Precinct responded to the scene.

Detective Sharp greeted Detective Moreno at the scene, saying, "This is horrible. Multiple homicide and the victims were torched to rid of the bodies."

"This location caters to all types of occult practitioners. I will check downstairs," Detective Moreno said.

Moreno poured oil in his hands and touched the entrance door. He walked to the basement and sensed extreme evil. He walked over to the bodies and looked at Vlad. Vlad opened his eyes, stood up, pulled the wooden stake from his chest, and charged at Detective Moreno, who fired three rounds into the chest of Vlad. The vampire dropped dead to the ground.

13

Detective Moreno Notes III

People become involved in the occult for power and control. We must understand that no one can develop psychic or occult powers. The term occult in Latin means *occultus* – knowledge that is hidden, secret, and mysterious. These powers come from demons that come into our bodies. These are not innate dormant powers that are developed through some ritual or ceremony. The rituals and ceremonies draw the attention of the specific demon or demons towards the occult practitioner, creating a destructive unity and relationship. Demons are not concerned for our well being, safety, or salvation. They only have one mission – to destroy humanity.

The vampire subculture is very popular today through videos, television, movies, books, the Internet, and role-playing games, such as Vampire: The Masquerade offers an endless array of information for those interested. Children as young as 5 years old are being exposed to such destructive information. Parents and guardians are oblivious to what their children are learning and being exposed to. The Internet can be the gateway to hell that leads children to the core of destruction. All types of predators patiently wait for children to log onto vampire, satanic, and occult websites. Information is our best defense to battle these predators and their demons.

The demon-possessed person will become physically possessed by the demon or demons. The afflicted person can have more than one demon inside of their body. The demonic host will control the mind and body of the possessed person. The demon will demonstrate abnormal physical strength, live in secluded areas and cemeteries, and inflict injury to the demon-possessed person.

> John 5:1 says, "Then they came to the other side of the sea, to the country of the Gadarenes. ²And when He had come out of the boat, immediately there met Him out of the tombs a man with an unclean spirit, ³who had *his* dwelling among the tombs; and no one could bind him, not even with chains, ⁴because he had often been bound with shackles and chains. And the chains had been pulled apart by him, and the shackles broken in pieces; neither could anyone tame him. ⁵And always, night and day, he was in the mountains and in the tombs, crying out and cutting himself with stones.
>
> "⁶When he saw Jesus from afar, he ran and worshiped Him. ⁷And he cried out with a loud voice and said, 'What have I to do with You, Jesus, Son of the Most High God? I implore you by God that you do not torment me.'
>
> "⁸For He said to him, 'Come out of the man, unclean spirit!' ⁹Then He asked him, 'What *is* your name?'
>
> "And he answered, saying, 'My name *is* Legion; for we are many.' ¹⁰Also he begged Him earnestly that He would not send them out of the country.
>
> "¹¹Now a large herd of swine was feeding there near the mountains. ¹²So all the demons begged Him, saying, 'Send us to the swine, that we may enter them.' ¹³And at once Jesus gave them permission. Then the unclean spirits went out and entered the swine (there were about two thousand); and the herd ran violently down the steep place into the sea, and drowned in the sea."

14

NYC College Student Overdose

Tony Anderson graduated from Columbia University in New York City as an honor student at the end of 2013. Originally from Minnesota, Tony was an only child, loved by his father Joseph, a grade foreman supervisor, and his mother Helen, a registered nurse. They were very lucky that Tony received a full scholarship to Columbia University for his hard work in high school. Tony wanted to complete his bachelor of science degree in earth and environmental engineering in hopes of working in New York City.

Tony met Sandra Jones in their sophomore year and planned to marry her after they both graduated. Sandra studied art history and archaeology. She hoped to work at the Metropolitan Museum of Art. They met while Tony played quarterback for the football team. They instantly fell in love and never looked at anyone else. They made a cute couple, being that Tony is six feet tall and she is five feet and seven inches. People said they were a perfect ten.

On Friday night, Tony, Sandra, Billy, and Sonny entered the La Madrina Club and Restaurant. The place was filled to capacity – they could feel the excitement with the music roaring through their chests. Tony regularly frequented the club and Pablo's men knew him. Tony spotted one of Pablo's men, Sammy, and they both walked to the bathroom. Tony and Sammy shook hands and Sammy slipped Tony a glassine envelope containing cocaine. Tony had a $100 dollar bill in his hand.

"Sammy," Tony said, "do you think I can buy a quarter kilo? People around me are asking, and I thought maybe we can work a good price."

"Yeah, let me inquire with my source. It is a good time to buy."

"How much?"

"Since we have known you for a year, and we know about your father Joseph and your mother Helen. They live at the corner red brick house on Sullivan Street. The price will be $15,500. We set up delivery, location, and security protocol. Only you will deliver the money."

Tony, shocked that they know about his parents, said, "Ok. Let me know when."

"Oh, we will. Consider this a done deal. We will call you soon."

Tony nervously walked back to Sandra and his friends. "Tony, what is wrong?" she asked.

"Nothing honey," he said. "I got it. Let's party." And they spent a couple of hours at the club. Tony felt very uneasy about the whole offer to buy from these people, but his greed to make money superseded his fears. He felt as if something was watching him – something devilish.

Late that evening, Tony drove Billy and Sammy to their apartments at 97th Street and Broadway. He and Sandra returned to his 110th Street and Riverside Drive apartment, which overlooked the Hudson River. As soon as he entered the apartment, he spread out the cocaine on a glass mirror on the living room table. He took out a straw from the kitchen, and Sandra brought him a Corona beer.

They both knelt on the floor in front of the living room table. Tony snorted two lines of cocaine and wiped his nose. Sandra took the straw and began to snort a line of cocaine when all of a sudden, Tony placed his hands on his head, gasping and screaming in pain. The pain in his head bent him over.

Sandra began to scream. Tony looked up and screamed, "Get away from me! Oh my God, help me!"

A tall figure penetrated the wall, causing Sandra to scream in horror. The figure was La Santa Muerte dressed in a black cloak. Her eyeless sockets stared at Tony. She grabbed him by the throat and snapped his neck, instantly killing him. Tony's lifeless body fell to the floor. La Santa Muerte grabbed Sandra and tossed her out the window, and she landed on a parked blue Ford. The crash made a horrifying sound, and people looked out their windows, screaming in horror. Many people immediately called 911.

The 26th Precinct Sector Adam Police Officers Michael Wright, John Sawyer, and Timothy Stryker, as well as Emergency Service Unit Sergeant William Doyle, responded to the apartment with their weapons drawn. Stryker broke down the door with a battering ram. As they rushed into the living room, Stryker screamed and Doyle fainted at the sight in front of them; Wright and Sawyer ran out of the apartment.

Two minutes later, Lieutenant Robert Hernandez walked into the apartment and picked up the glassine envelope, which had a skeleton face on it. Having attended an occult class taught by Detective Mark Moreno previously, Hernandez called police headquarters and asked Moreno for assistance in the case. Moreno immediately prayed to Jesus Christ to give him the wisdom and skill to investigate this possible occult crime and bring the perpetrator or perpetrators to justice. He held his Bible close to his heart, breathing in and out. He placed the Bible in his bag and left his office.

Twenty minutes later, after Moreno arrived in front of apartment 21 and showed his identification, he poured oil on his hands. He touched the sides of the door and said, "Jesus Christ, I pray in your name that the Holy Spirit enlightens me with wisdom and understanding to analyze this crime scene. In your name, I expel all demonic spirits to leave this crime scene that the Holy Spirit may reveal the truth, amen." As Moreno walked into the apartment, he felt a demonic force move away from him, departing the apartment completely.

The crime scene unit signaled Moreno to come in. Hernandez greeted him and showed the glassine envelope. "This is bad, Mark, real bad. The apartment was locked from the inside, and no prints were found. We had to scrape the female from the car hood. She was thrown with great force out the window. When I came in, there was an eerie feeling in the room and the smell of sulfur. What or who could have done this to these kids? I do not want to know. The crime scene is yours."

In the middle of the living room was the headless body of Tony with his severed arms next to his body. Tony's head was placed on top of his chest, facing his feet; his eyes had been removed and were nowhere to be found. The body was inside a circle burned into the living room floor, illumined by a black candle. The black candle had a black skull printed in the glass.

Detective Moreno sprinkled oil and water at the crime scene, praying, "Lord Jesus, I glorify you as I humble myself gathering the crime scene information. I pray that each element identifies those responsible for this crime." All of a sudden, the glassine envelope flew from Moreno's hand and landed on the floor. Moreno realized that the envelope identified the suspects. This crime was not committed by one person, but by a group of people involved in a specific occult practice.

A week later, the forensic report concluded that Tony had died of a cocaine-induced overdose. Cocaine creates a euphoric effect on the brain, causing a "rush" feeling. Powdered cocaine can be snorted, or even injected into the veins if mixed with water. Physiological effects include increased blood pressure and heart rate, dilated pupils, insomnia, and loss of appetite.

In the case of Tony, the cocaine was mixed with peyote. Peyote is a spineless cactus that contains the ingredient of the hallucinogen mescaline. Mescaline causes illusions, hallucinations, altered perception of space and time, and altered body image. According to the DEA, peyote and mescaline are Schedule 1 substances under the Controlled Substance Act. Peyote and mescaline have a high potential for abuse among users with no medical use in the United States.

Detective Moreno suspected that the combinations of cocaine, peyote, and mescaline opened the mind of Tony to demon contact. When an individual brings his brain frequency to a certain state, the brain is open to demons or demon to enter. The demon came to

Tony and killed Sandra and ritualistically murdered Tony as a sacrifice. Tony didn't experience illusions or hallucinations, but an actual encounter with a powerful demon. Moreno just needed to identify which demon this was and the meaning of the skeleton face on the glassine envelope.

Drug users do not realize that many drugs will open the gateway to hell and demonic forces will torment your lives, and ultimately kill you after you have destroyed the lives of family and friends. Once these demons destroy you, they leave to torment others. The secular world will not accept the fact that Satan and demons exist only to create chaos, torture, torment, and death. This is spiritual warfare at its worse.

15

Hell in Times Square

Early Friday morning at Pablo's residence, he held a meeting with his people about the night's activities. Pablo thanked his people for the success of the operation. La Niña Club was becoming one of the most popular sites in the city of New York.

"I have a small run for tonight for 96ᵗʰ Street," Pablo started. "Octavio, I want you and Pepe to hand-deliver a half a kilo of cocaine to the Hernandez brothers at 201 West 96ᵗʰ Street off Broadway and Riverside Drive."

"No problem. Any backup?"

"No. Keep it tight and carry your weapons. The Hernandez brothers wired the money. Pepe, you drive the SUV and do not stop at any point going and coming."

"Ok, boss."

"May La Santa Muerte protect you both."

At 6:00 P.M., Pablo handed Octavio a locked black attaché case. Pepe drove west, with Octavio riding shotgun. Traffic picked up on 42ⁿᵈ Street and Madison Avenue. Pepe drove in the left lane on 44ᵗʰ Street and Madison Avenue, when suddenly a black Toyota in the right lane turned left in front of Pepe's SUV, causing Pepe to swerve right and run through the red light signal, almost causing an accident with oncoming cars.

Police Officer Juan Sanchez observed Pepe run the red light. He approached Pepe's stopped vehicle as his partner, Police Officer Michael Doyle, walked over to the passenger side. Octavio held his

9mm weapon close to his chest in his left hand. As Doyle approached the door, Octavio fired one shot at PO Doyle and missed. Pepe sped off west on 45th Street from Madison Avenue. Sanchez and Doyle ran to their vehicles and pursued the SUV.

"10-13! 10-13!" Doyle yelled over radio. "Shots fired. Two Hispanic males in black SUV, tag number Eddie Oscar Henry 8015, heading west on 45 Street and Madison Avenue. 10-13!"

Central responded: "10-04. All available units, 10-13; black SUV, two Hispanics, male, armed, heading westbound on 45th Street."

"What do we do?" Pepe asked, panicking.

"Shut up and drive!" Octavio pointed his gun out of his vehicle window and fired at the police car. NYPD vehicles followed Sanchez's vehicle. Pepe kept driving as fast as he could down 45th Street. An NYPD aviation helicopter followed from above; the media monitored the NYPD radio frequency.

When Pepe reached Broadway, he made a sharp left turn, losing control of the car, which rear-ended a blue Ford waiting for the traffic light to change. The driver smashed his head against his steering wheel, totally knocked out.

Pepe and Octavio, shaken, jumped out of their vehicle with guns drawn and ran into a crowd of people. Sanchez and Doyle followed closely behind, their weapons at the ready. Pepe and Octavio turned left onto 44th Street and leaned on the building around the corner for the officers. As Sanchez turned on 44th Street, Octavio fired, striking Sanchez point-blank in the chest. Doyle shot at Octavio and missed. Octavio fired back at Doyle, striking him in the shoulder. Sanchez, still aiming his gun, shot Pepe in the right leg. Pepe fell to the ground, and Octavio ran east on 44th Street.

Sanchez yelled over the radio, "10-13! Officers shot, 10-13!" Within minutes, police swarmed the scene from Midtown North, Midtown South, 19th, and 20th Precincts. They cuff Pepe, who was transported to Bellevue Hospital.

At the crime scene, Emergency Service Unit Sergeant McNamara checked the perpetrators' vehicle. In the front passenger side, he found a black attaché case containing hundreds of glassine envelopes, all of which carried a white substance. Each envelope was stamped with a red skeletal face.

The next morning, Pepe awoke cuffed to his bed. Midtown North Precinct Detective Quinn and Detective Moreno stood next to the bed. Pepe is drowsy from the leg surgery.

"How are you feeling?" Detective Quinn asked.

"I am in pain, idiota!"

"You're the idiot cuffed to the bed."

Moreno waved Quinn to be silent.

"You do not understand," Pepe said. "She is going to find you. Nothing is going to protect you."

"Who is going to find us?" Moreno responded.

"Let me go, let me go!"

"Calm down, my man. Calm down."

"We are going to read you your rights," said Quinn.

"I do not need my rights. Rights for what?" Pepe laughed.

Moreno leaned toward Pepe's right side and said, "I notice you have a skeleton figure tattoo on your back."

"Leave it alone and go away from this situation. She will avenge us. La Negrita is coming," Pepe snapped.

Quinn laughed. "Oh, stop this B.S. La Negrita or whatever you call it does not exist. Give me a break!"

"What do you know, you waste of human life!" Pepe spat.

Quinn grabbed Pepe by the chin; Moreno intervened by pushing Quinn out of the way, asking, "Are you involved with La Santa Muerte?"

"She is torturing me! Help me!" Pepe screamed.

Demon possession occurs for various reasons. People become possessed by dabbling in the occult, demonology, Satanism, voodoo, etc. and being cursed by someone. You can inherit a curse from relatives from two or three centuries ago. Demons may lie dormant inside of a person before manifesting itself.

Demons can cause blindness, epilepsy, paralysis mental illness, speaking in a foreign language never studied by the possessed person, and physical strength. Many occult experts believe you can see the demon through the person's eyes. The Bible illustrated many demon possessions cured by Jesus Christ.

The face of Pepe turned into La Santa Muerte and growled at Moreno, screaming, "I will kill you!"

Detective Rivera walked into the room and looked at Pepe. He fainted.

Moreno began to pray to Jesus Christ to expel the demon from Pepe.

"Pepe, listen to me and call on the name of Jesus Christ."

Pepe's face came back as he called on the name of Jesus Christ.

La Santa Muerte yelled, "Pablo will avenge me!"

Pepe screamed, "Jesus, help me!" and fainted.

Moreno tapped Pepe's face. "Wake up! Who is Pablo?"

Pepe, awake, began to cry. "Pablo is my godfather in the religion."

Moreno nodded, finally understanding.

The elevator stopped on their floor and two men dressed in janitor uniforms exited. One of the men pushed a cart filled with brooms and cleaning items. The other removed a Mac-10 with a silencer and shot the police guard outside Pepe's room. Hearing the thud, Detective Doyle came out of the room and charged Pablo's two men, Memo and Jesus, who both kicked him in the head, knocking him out.

Detective Moreno shot the first suspect by the door.

Memo's weapon jammed; Moreno kicked the weapon out of his hand. Memo countered with a left hook, which was blocked by Moreno, who then kicked the suspect in the stomach. He grabbed the suspect by the head and waist, and slammed him into the wall, knocking him out and cuffing him.

After picking up Rivera from the ground and placing him on a chair, Moreno ran into the hospital room to find Pepe resting on his bed. The exorcism had worked.

"I am going to help you with this situation," Moreno said. "Help us fight against Pablo and his cult. God Almighty will protect you; I assure you of that."

"Ok, I do not want family in Mexico to suffer for my mistake." "I will not allow you or your family to suffer."

"No quiero murir."

"You now live forever because Jesus Christ lives in you as your lord and savior. This happened for a reason."

When Pepe was initiated into La Santa Muerte religion, the initiation opened a portal that allowed La Santa Muerte access to possess Pepe. During the exorcism, La Santa Muerte manifested itself in the body of Pepe as witnessed in the hospital.

The reality of demon possession torments all societies at an alarming rate. Many cases of demon possession are misdiagnosed as mental illness, even though many cases demonstrate similar characteristics. Secular and sinful society denies the existence of demon possession. This attitude is based on ignorance and denial. This allows Satan and his demons to operate freely in the world to corrupt and destroy mankind.

Unfortunately, many individuals associate with Satan and demons. The truth about Satan and demons involves their ability to disguise themselves as spirits, gods, goddesses, and benevolent angels. The Bible says that Satan disguises himself as an angel of light. The devil desires that we do not believe that he does not exist.

16

Detective Moreno Meets with Pastor Rivera

Detective Moreno conducted research in his office, and he loved reading and writing. He believed in reading material written by occult practitioners and not by experts because practitioners are coming directly from their experiences, emotions, and perceptions. The telephone in his office rang.

"Detective Moreno, may I help you?"

"Hi, it is Pastor Rivera. How are you?"

"Hi. God Bless. I am well, and you?"

"Good, praise God. I am calling about tonight's deliverance service. Are you still coming?"

"Yes I am."

"See you then, Detective."

After replacing the receiver, Moreno picked up his Bible and read John 8:44: "Ye are of your father the Devil, and the lusts of your father ye will do. He was a murderer from the beginning, and abode not in the truth, because there is no truth in him. When he speaks a lie, he speaks of his own: for he is a liar, and the father of it."

The Devil is a liar because he convinces people that one does not need Jesus Christ in their lives as their personal lord and savior. Satan assigned La Santa Muerte to Mexico to destroy people that worship her. In reality, demons do not have sexual gender as male and female. According to the Bible, angels and demons are masculine in gender.

This is not an insult to the feminine gender that blesses God's creation. God Almighty created Eve last because God saved the best for last.

At 6:30 P.M., Moreno left his office and drove to 300 Flatbush Avenue, Christ Deliverance Church. The church was filled with over sixty practitioners singing and praising God. Moreno, greeted by Pastor Rivera, approached the pulpit dressed in a pastoral collar. It is amazing that Detective Moreno represents the government of God as a law enforcement officer.

Pastor Raul Rivera, born in New York City, lived in Spanish Harlem with his parents Maria and Raul and sisters, Maria and Minerva. He attended Hunter College and at the age of 25, Jesus touched his heart to become a pastor. In 2004, he opened the Christ Deliverance Church. He met Detective Moreno at the New York City Police Academy while attending the Citizens Police Academy Program. Moreno had been conducting the class about Cult/Occult Awareness. Jesus Christ brought them together and they have been brothers in Christ ever since.

Every Wednesday, at 7:00 P.M., Pastor Rivera conducted deliverance services. Deliverance is a Christian term meaning that Christians will pray and put their hands on a person that needs physical, mental, spiritual healing, specifically, demon possession, and demon oppression. Most people do not know that a demon or demons will possess or oppress them. Deliverance refers to conducting an exorcism of demons and Satan. Exorcisms require prayer and fasting unless the exorcism must be done suddenly.

Pastor Rivera began the service with Detective Moreno standing at the pulpit. Moreno assisted these services as a Christian without representing the New York City Police Department. Pastor Rivera said, "I pray the Lord Jesus Christ that the Holy Spirit fills Christian Deliverance Church and our hearts, and reveals anyone needing deliverance from demons, the occult, witchcraft, sorcery, spells, and curses. Anyone in need of deliverance, please step forward."

Men, woman, and children began to line up in front of the pulpit. Moreno stood to the right of Pastor Rivera. For the next ninety minutes, people were healed of their physical, mental, financial, and spiritual ills. Many accepted Jesus Christ as their personal lord and savior. Pastor Rivera and Detective Moreno poured oil and prayed for them. Moreno loved this line of work.

At the end of the line stood a black woman, wearing a black dress and a brown jacket. She stared at the floor as she approached Pastor Rivera and Detective Moreno. Moreno placed his left hand on her forehead and prayed. The Holy Spirit revealed to him that the woman is demon-possessed through her occult practice of sorcery.

"In the name of Jesus Christ," Detective Moreno said, "I expel you, demon, from this child of Christ." The woman fell to the ground and began sizzling and crawling as a snake. Everyone around her ran back, praying intensely. Pastor Rivera grabbed a bottle of oil. The woman began to crawl up the wall of the church. In horror, many children screamed and one woman in the front row fainted. Pastor Rivera grabbed her leg and she kicked him in the chest, sending him flying.

Detective Moreno grabbed her by the legs and pulled her to the ground. Her skin appeared scaly, like a snake. He poured oil on her head and she growled in pain. Her face resembled a snake with red eyes. Dazed, Pastor Rivera came over to assist Moreno, who had realized this present situation became a matter of life and death.

The woman said, "I am in pain. Stop tormenting me!"

"What is your name, Miss?"

"My name is Estelle. Help me!"

The demon yelled, "Shut the hell up!"

Detective Moreno asked, "Demon, what is your name?"

"My name is Aida Wedo, the Lwa of water, snakes and the rainbow, represented by the rainbow python."

Detective Moreno sprinkled oil upon Estelle's head and yelled, "In the name of Jesus Christ through his precious blood, I expel you, demon snake, back to hell!"

Estelle growled and screamed while the congregation prayed out loud.

"Estelle, can you hear me?" Her skin became normal.

"Yes, help me, please."

"I command you Demon. Leave in the name of Jesus! Estelle, do you accept Jesus Christ as your personal lord and savior?"

The demon yelled, "Leave her alone! She is mine!"

"Fire, fire, fire!" Pastor Rivera yelled. "I pray fire from the Holy Spirit to come down and burn you, demon."

The demon squealed in pain, causing the children in the church to hold on tight to their parents.

Estelle faints.

Moreno poured the jar of oil on the head of Estelle. The demon screamed.

"Estelle, do you accept Jesus Christ as your lord and savior?" Estelle screamed for five minutes as Moreno and Pastor Rivera prayed.

For two minutes, Estelle remained silent. Then, crying, she called on Jesus Christ! She stood up and yelled, "Jesus, you are my lord and savior! I love you. I love you."

The congregation applauded and called out the name of Jesus Christ.

Moreno asked Estelle to come up to the podium and talk about her testimony.

Estelle said, "Five years ago, I became involved with voodoo as a high priestess and gave my soul to Aida Wedo. People paid me to curse others and bless them with success. I loved hurting and killing with black magic from my home altar. This religion hurt my family and made me reject them and anything related to Christianity. I opposed everything related to Christianity.

"Now I live for Jesus Christ as my personal lord and savior. I was walking by the church and God led me inside these doors. God works in wondrous ways. I have so much to learn. Praise you, Jesus."

Detective Moreno said, "Tonight, I want you to go home with a group from the church and physically destroy the altar. Place the broken items in bags and throw them out. The church will bless your home with oil and bring you the peace of God Almighty, Jesus Christ, and the Holy Spirit. Amen." The congregation applauded.

After the service, Moreno met with Pastor Rivera in his church office.

Pastor Rivera said, "Thank you for coming."

"My pleasure. This is for the Lord Jesus' glory. Pastor, I have discovered a Mexican cocaine-trafficking cult operating in New York City. They are involved in La Santa Muerte religion. They are stamping their glassine envelopes with a red skeletal face representing La Santa Muerte. This is demonic and will destroy the lives of hundreds of people, including teenagers. I will fight them with all my power in the name of Jesus Christ."

Pastor Rivera answered, "The Holy Spirit has a word of wisdom for you. He wants you to know, 'Your enemies will come after you and surround you, but I will protect you and destroy their plan of destruction against you and my children in Jesus' name.'"

"Amen, my Lord," Moreno responded. "Your words are accepted as true as God is truth. All I want, Jesus, is wisdom to perform thy will. Thank you, Lord, for all you continue to do in my life. Amen."

"Let us pray. Jesus, bless and protect with your precious blood my brother Mark Moreno in his personal and professional life that involves exposing Satan for the liar that he is. He fights a spiritual warfare within the New York City Police Department being the only cop that patrols the dark side. Amen."

"Amen. Nice seeing you, my brother Rivera."

"Same here."

17

Pepe's Arraignment at Manhattan Criminal Court

Pepe sat handcuffed in his wheelchair with his attorney Richard Valdez sitting on his right side. Detective Moreno sat in the back of the courtroom. Judge Rodulovic presided at the bench. Pepe looked behind at Moreno and they both smiled.

Bond is set for $1 million and Pepe's attorney argued that the bond is too high for a man that only drove a vehicle and was handed a weapon unknown to his client by a male passenger.

"Your Honor, my client has no prior arrest and was asked by a co-worker to drive him to Midtown."

District Attorney Gonzales said, "He is a Mexican national that can flee the States."

"Are you kidding? How? You expect my client to perform cartwheels through the Mexican border?"

Everyone in the courtroom laughed, including Judge Rodulovic waved his hand for silence and started, "Let me…"

Suddenly, a black winged creature resembling a lizard crashed through the window and stood between the judge's bench and Pepe's table. Everyone screamed in horror. The two court officers radioed for help and the creature slammed the both of them across the wall. People began to stampede out of the court room.

Pepe's attorney ran for his life out of the courtroom yelling, "I do not think so!" The creature growled at Pepe, who fell from his wheelchair, screaming. As the creature walked toward Pepe, Detective Moreno fired his weapon, striking the creature several times in the chest. The wounded creature hovered overhead and Detective Moreno reloaded and fired.

The creature fell into the front court benches and Moreno continued to fire his weapon. Court officers entered the courtroom with weapons drawn. The creature crawled on the ground like a snake with wings flapping. The creature died and turned to dust. Everyone in the courtroom shook with fear.

Detective Moreno ran over to Pepe, lifting him up and placing him on the wheelchair. The court officers wheeled Pepe back into the cells. Moreno holstered his weapon and sat down. He thought that this demon was sent to kill Pepe, but God Almighty protected him. Pepe was a threat to Pablo and the demon La Santa Muerte. This situation had become critical. No one was safe, including the cult members who betrayed Pablo and the demon.

Court Officer Stein told Detective Moreno that Judge Rodulovic wanted to see him in chambers.

As Moreno entered the room, Judge Rodulovic poured himself a drink, saying, "What was that thing in my courtroom?"

"Do you really want to know, your Honor?"

"Not really. But that thing caused havoc in my courtroom. I have never seen or experienced anything like this."

"Your Honor, that thing was a demon sent by someone to kill Pepe Santiago. You experienced the worse type of black magic anyone can perform. This was committed by a black magician working with the power of hell."

Judge Rodulovic took another drink. "I thought these things only existed in the movies."

Moreno chuckled.

Judge Rodulovic said, "What do I do now in this case?"

"Schedule the next stage for a few months and allow me to deal with the source of that demon."

"You know the source of this evilness?"

"Yes I do. All I can say is that the source comes from Mexico."

"Holy Christ, Detective. How can these people be allowed to do what they do? This frightens me on many different levels."

"Read the Bible, your Honor, and live by its words. You represent justice that God Almighty has established. I need to interrogate Pepe and have him turn state's evidence against Pablo and all his people. I believe Pablo has committed murders in Mexico before coming to New York City."

"I will talk to the district attorney and set up a meeting with Pepe and his attorney."

"Thank you, your Honor."

"Thank you. It has been the strangest day in my life, a day I do not want to ever experience again."

"Thank you, sir. Goodbye."

"Keep me in tune."

"I will."

Two days later, Detective Moreno met with Assistant District Attorney Pedro Gonzales, Attorney Valdez, and Police Officer Torres at 60 Court Street. Detective Moreno poured oil in his hands and rubbed them on the front door of the office and the windows. No demons would come through this office today.

"Mr. Valdez," Moreno started, "I liked the way you ran out of the courtroom."

"You're real funny, detective. I wasn't waiting for that thing to have me for lunch."

"All you had to do was to confront it and throw few punches."

"Yeah, right. I left it up to you and your cop friends. I don't get paid that much."

Detective Moreno laughed.

Gonzales said, "I'd like to offer your client a deal: misdemeanor on the gun charge if he gives up the operation."

Pepe and his attorney spoke for a few minutes before his lawyer said, "I do not want my client testifying in open court and the same deal with the Mexican authorities."

"We will talk to the State Department and the Mexican authorities, but we can only promise you the outcome of this case if your client's information is valid."

Pepe and his attorney spoke again briefly.

"Ok. We want the deal in writing. My client will give up everything he knows about Pablo, his operation, and crimes committed."

Gonzales said, "Deal," and they shook hands.

Detective Moreno silently prayed. "Thank you, Jesus, for bringing us together. I pray the the Holy Spirit enlighten us and speak through Pepe with the truth and bring all guilty parties to justice in Jesus' name." He then spent two hours questioning Pepe about Pablo's entire operation and La Santa Muerte. It was critical for Detective Moreno to understand the interactive, dedicated relationship Pablo had with La Santa Muerte. This indicated Pablo's defense mechanisms and tactics against anyone, including law enforcement, attempting to disrupt his relationship with La Santa Muerte. This information would assist Detective Moreno in developing a course of action to confront, arrest, and bring to justice Pablo and his men – and destroy La Santa Muerte.

Pepe and Detective Moreno shook hands and hugged each other at the end of questioning.

"Listen, my brother, I will do everything in Jesus' name to help you and your family. Christ is with you forever. God Almighty will help me take down this demon."

With tears in his eyes, Pepe said, "Thank you, hermano. I thought I was dead, lost, and forgotten. But thanks to Jesus, he rescued me."

"Amen. See you soon."

18

Armageddon in New York City

Back at 1 Police Plaza, Detective Moreno reviewed the case. He prayed as he sat in his chair. "Lord Jesus, thank you for my involvement in this case involving drug trafficking, murder, and demonology. This case comes to an end and I hope there is no further violence. But if Pablo, with the aid of La Santa Muerte, chooses violence, be my shield and protector, my Lord. Help me with the best tactics and strategies to eliminate the threat. I ask this for your glory, my lord and savior. Amen."

Two weeks into the surveillance, Detective Moreno entered La Niña Club and Restaurant and sat at the bar, ordering cranberry juice. He watched Octavio giving orders to the men working inside; he watched Maria dealing drugs. She was always surrounded by two bodyguards.

From the bar, Detective Moreno observed Pablo standing a few feet away, talking to a group of people. Pablo's hands began to shake; he rubbed them together. He felt uncomfortable because La Santa Muerte within him felt the Holy Spirit inside Detective Moreno.

For the next two weeks, Detective Moreno listened to the cult's phone calls, took photographs, and conducted surveillance of La Niña Club and Restaurant. He followed Pablo's men on their errands. No matter how close Moreno came to them, they never suspected him.

He showed the photographs to the detectives handling the 44th Street and Broadway incident and the responding police officers involved. Two weeks prior, Pepe identified Octavio Baez as the shooter during the ADA interview. At 7:00 A.M. the next day, a warrant was issued for the arrest of Octavio. An Emergency Service Unit, Detective Cortez, and Detective Moreno met at Midtown North Precinct to discuss the arrest.

"Octavio lives at 430 West 160th Street, apartment 3D," Cortez said. "He lives alone."

"He is dangerous and heavily armed and will go down with a fight," Moreno picked up. "When he is arrested, do not allow him to use the phone until we arrest Pablo and his men. These people practice hardcore magic. They have everything to lose. So let's be careful."

ESU Sergeant James Molloy pulled Detective Moreno to the side. "Is it true these people worship the Devil?"

"No. They worship a demon called La Santa Muerte."

"Should I worry? Will I be cursed?"

"No. Are you Catholic?"

"Yes, I am."

"Believe in God and all will be fine."

"Ok. Thanks."

At 8:10 A.M., the team arrived at 159th Street. The ESU ran into the building to the third floor and stood in front of apartment 3D. ESU Police Officer Smith slammed the door open with his battering ram and the team entered the apartment.

A gun appeared out of a hallway door and fired at the EDU officers. Smith was shot in the leg and dropped to the ground. Memo and Jose opened fire at the ESU team members from the doorway. The ESU returned gunfire, striking and killing the two criminals.

Octavio crashed through the living room window to the fire escape and ran up the steps toward the roof. Detective Moreno followed him; when he reached the roof, Octavio opened fire at him. Moreno concealed himself behind the stairwell. Octavio ran to edge of the west side of the building and leapt the four feet to the next building's roof, landing safely.

Detective Moreno followed and ran after Octavio, tackling him before Octavio reached the stairway. Octavio swung a right hook and missed; and Detective Moreno shoulder-dropped him to the ground. He turned Octavio over and cuffed him.

Laughing, Octavio said, "You think you will find Pablo? He is gone!"

"What do you mean?"

"He is gone, stupid. Never to be found."

"Gee, I am stupid and you are in cuffs."

This information didn't surprise Moreno because Pablo has connections in high places. The only place Pablo would go back to is Mexico City. After rushing Octavio back to Midtown Precinct, Moreno met with the ESU team, ready to execute the arrest of Pablo. Upon reaching La Niña Club and Restaurant, the janitor told them that Pablo had left and would return the following week. Detective Moreno knew that Pablo and the rest of his cult members would not return to New York City.

19

The Final Battle

Detective Moreno immediately called CIA Supervisor Stevens to explain the situation and Pablo's escape. Supervisor Stevens said, "Let me check with our database for outgoing private planes leaving the United States, and I will call you back."

"Thank you, sir."

"Listen, Mark. My daughter is healthy again right after I accepted Jesus Christ."

"Please Praise God Almighty."

After hanging up the phone, Detective Moreno loaded his vehicle with weapons to confront the ultimate enemy. He read Psalm 23: "The Lord *is* my shepherd; I shall not want. Yea, though I walk through the valley of the shadow of death, I will fear no evil..." Detective Moreno feared no one because the Lord Jesus Christ protects him.

An hour later, Stevens called back. "Hey. I have the information. A Jet Star Charter jet left from La Guardia Airport an hour ago. The jet was headed to Mexico City. I can have a jet ready for you and a three-man backup team. Our contacts in Mexico will supply support." "Thank you. I am going with the goal of bringing him back dead or alive. Pablo is very violent and depends on La Santa Muerte for strength. He will not go down easy, but hard."

"Be careful."

"I need to talk to you about my role in the agency."

"Let's have a face-to-face ASAP."

"Cool."

Five hours and thirty-seven minutes later, Detective Moreno landed at a private airfield thirty miles west of Mexico City. He held the Bible in his right hand as the private jet stopped. The door opened and he was immediately met by CIA Operative Manuel Soto.

"Welcome to Mexico City."

"Thank you."

"This is Victor and William."

Everyone shook hands and then headed to a black SUV. The SUV was bullet- and grenade-proof with tinted windows.

"We traced Pablo and his people to a heavily fenced house in New Polanco area of Mexico City," Manuel said. "He arrived a few hours ago and has not left. Strange, but he rolled this black-veiled seven-foot box on wheels into the house. We do not know its contents."

Detective Moreno knew that the black-veiled box contained the stone statue of La Santa Muerte. Statues of idols contain the demonic spirit or spirits inside of them. It does not matter if the statue is made of stone, mud, cement, or concrete. Bringing a statue to your home causes the demon or demons to create havoc, destruction, devastation, and death to the occupants.

In the case of the statue of La Santa Muerte, this powerful demon converted and materialized the stone into her demonic bones, able to move around on Earth. Pablo and his followers didn't have the slightest hint of the danger in which they had placed themselves and those around them. Detective Moreno suspected that someone was behind the power behind Pablo's throne. Who could that be? He would surely find out.

The SUV entered the U.S. Embassy and the officers quickly entered the Situation Room, which housed satellite surveillance and computer databases. Detective Moreno loved the Situation Room and all its instruments. He thanked Jesus Christ Almighty for the opportunity in his calling for God – spiritual warfare.

For the next hour, they planned the black operation and Detective Moreno understood that Pablo needed to be brought back dead or alive. This would get bloody and people would die. La Santa Muerte would be destroyed! She persuaded the good people of Mexico into thinking she was good and caring. According to the Bible, death exists as physical and spiritual death. We all die physically, but spiritual death occurs when you do not accept Jesus Christ as your personal lord and savior.

Physical death is the separation of one's spirit and the body. Spiritual death is separation from God Almighty, Jesus Christ, and the Holy Spirit.

> "This (his body) is the bread which cometh down from heaven, that a man may eat thereof, and not die. I am the living bread which came down from heaven: if any man eat of this bread, he shall live forever: and the bread that I will give is my flesh, which I will give for the life of the world." John 6.50–51

> "He that hath the Son hath life; and he that hath not the Son of God hath not life." 1 John 5.12

Jesus Christ offers eternal life to those that accept him as lord and savior. No one can take us away from Jesus Christ. Jesus does not want us to die in our sins. Hell was made for those who reject Jesus Christ: "And I give unto them eternal life; and they shall never perish, neither shall any man pluck them out of my hand" (John 10.28). Those who abide in him will never see spiritual death:

> "Verily, verily, I say unto you, if a man keep my saying, he shall never see death." John 8.51

> "Then said Jesus again unto them, I go my way, and ye shall seek me, and shall die in your sins: whither I go, ye cannot come...I said therefore unto you, that ye shall die in your sins: for if ye believe not that I am he, ye shall die in your sins." John 8.21–24

At 2:00 A.M., Detective Moreno and his team arrived at Pablo's hideout location. From the SUV, Soto electronically turned off Pablo's house alarm. Pablo and his people hid in the two-story fenced complex. Moreno and his team scaled the adjacent building and roped down onto Pablo's roof. Soto opened the roof door and they entered. Moreno and Soto went to the left. In the hallway, they encountered Luis, who pulled his weapon and Detective Moreno fired, killing Luis.

Jesus heard the thump on the floor and yelled, "Intruders!" Running footsteps were heard throughout the house; Victor and William were soon greeted with gunfire. They took cover against the wall and returned fire. Tito came from behind, slashing William in the back; William fell to the ground. Victor and Tito fall to the ground, scuffling, and Tito stabbed Victor in the right shoulder. Detective Moreno and Soto fired at Tito, who dropped dead.

Detective Moreno saw three people run across the main floor into a doorway. Jesus fired his automatic weapon at Moreno and his team ducked for cover.

"Plan two is in effect," Detective Moreno said to Soto. "Take the team back to the SUV and meet me at location two."

"Good luck and may God be with you."

Detective Moreno stood guard until the team left.

As soon as the team cleared the area, Detective Moreno came downstairs and stood by the locked basement door. He placed an explosive charge on the door and breached the door open. When the smoke cleared, he noticed that the room is the La Santa Muerte altar. He could feel through the Holy Spirit the evilness and demonic forces inside the room. Immediately, he thought of Psalms 23:4. "Yea, though I walk through the valley of the shadow of death, I will fear no evil."

Detective Moreno observed that the square altar room was approximately fifty-by-fifty feet. The white walls were lined with red and black candles. Wooden chairs and a cluttered table faced the altar and the statue of La Santa Muerte. Behind the altar was a closed door.

Detective Moreno ran into the altar room behind a huge freight box. He listened intently to voices coming from behind the statue, weapon in hand.

"Pablo, you made a big mistake that will cost you your life."

"I do not think so. I was going to take you down and slice you in half."

Holding his weapon, Jesus stuck his head out from behind La Santa Muerte, and Moreno fired, striking Jesus in the head.

Pablo looked at Jesus and closed his eyes, beginning to silently pray to La Santa Muerte.

"Hey," he called out when he was finished. "Detective Moreno. I give up. Look. I am throwing my weapon out."

Pablo raised his arms and walked away from La Santa Muerte. Detective Moreno cautiously stepped toward Pablo. Pablo knelt, closing his eyes and praying. "My Lady, I pray that you give me strength and power to end the life of this menace to your kingdom. Detective Moreno must die a painful death and be sent down into your torturous dungeon. Allow me to serve you and fulfill this prophecy."

Pablo opened his mouth and screamed; La Santa Muerte became alive in spirit form and entered into Pablo's mouth. Pablo's face turned into the skeletal face of La Santa Muerte. He stood up and stared with red bulging eyes at Detective Moreno.

Detective Moreno sternly faced La Santa Muerte, bowing his head and silently praying, "Lord Jesus, my savior, I pray at this moment for you to be my shield, strength, and fortress. Defeat this demon with your precious blood, and destroy her hold on Pablo. Put an end to this demon's hold on the city of New York, and send La Santa Muerte back to hell. I humbly ask this for your glory. Amen."

Pablo threw two fast punches with one arm, catching Detective Moreno in the face. He returned a solid kick to Pablo's head, snapping his head back, and moving Pablo back five feet. Pablo charged Moreno and knocked him down. As they both rolled on the ground, Moreno stood, placing Pablo into a headlock and punching Pablo's face five times. Pablo shoved Moreno into a wall.

Pablo picked up the altar dagger from the ground and swung it wildly at Detective Moreno. Moreno quickly stepped out of the way of the deadly blows. He grabbed Pablo's right arm and flipped him to the ground. Pablo picked up trash from the floor, tossing it at Detective Moreno's face, temporarily blinding him. Pablo stood and raised the dagger over his head, lunging at Detective Moreno. Moreno took out his FN 5.7-caliber Herstal and fired three shots into Pablo, killing him instantly.

Suddenly Maria, in a black dress, floated through the air from the door behind the altar, and landed next to Pablo's dead body. The spirit of La Santa Muerte rushed out of Pablo's body and entered Maria's mouth. Her face turned into the skeletal face of La Santa Muerte with eyeless sockets and large sharp teeth.

Growling, La Santa Muerte said, "Your time has ended, servant of the man from Galilee. I will take you to hell tonight after I torture and kill you."

"In the name of Jesus Christ through his precious blood," Detective Moreno responded, "I expel you out of Maria and send you back to hell."

Maria growled in pain, "La Santa Muerte is my Lady, and I reject Jesus Christ! I am the power behind Pablo's success. He was just a sacrifice blinded by power and greed. Before he killed Raul, Raul initiated me as the Queen to rule through La Santa Muerte. My Lady made me the woman that I am. Pablo never knew the truth because the truth was bigger than he was."

"Neither you nor Pablo, Raul, or your men knew the truth because the truth is Jesus Christ. He would have set you free from sin and involvement with the demon of death, La Santa Muerte. Repent or die!"

"You will die!"

Maria picked up the sword and charged Detective Moreno, who emptied his weapon into her body. The sword dropped from her hand as she stumbled to the ground. As Maria lay dead next to Pablo, La Santa Muerte exited her body and crouched on the floor, staring at Moreno. She appeared to be losing power and strength. Moreno took the sword in his right hand and stabbed the heart of La Santa Muerte. He pulled the sword out of her heart, and struck her in the neck, removing her skeletal head. Her headless body fell to the ground and began to burn.

Detective Moreno dropped to his knees. "Thank you, Jesus. Thank you so much."

Soto rushed into the room. "Are you alright?

"Yes. No problem. Let us leave."

Six hours later, Detective Moreno was at home with his lovely wife Lynette and his son Gabriel. He held them in his arm with tears in his eyes.

"Dad, what is wrong?"

"I love you guys so much and I thank Jesus Christ for the both of you."

"I love you too, Dad. Promise me you will never die because I could not live without you."

"I promise I will always stay safe. Jesus Christ will always protect me."

Lynette looked at Moreno with tears in her eyes because she loved him so much.

Moreno cleared his throat. "Ok, guys. Let us have a blessed lunch and a beautiful day."

Lynette and Gabriel say, "Amen."

I want to thank you Jesus for your VICTORY. AMEN.

20

Conclusion

Many people needlessly died in the hands of Pablo Cruz. He knowingly decided to follow La Santa Muerte in his quest for power at the cost of his life. Blinded by his greed, he never realized that the real leader of the cult was Maria. Pablo was only a sacrifice for La Santa Muerte.

The demon La Santa Muerte deceived everyone in her path and continues to influence the hearts of the Mexican people searching for truth and salvation, including Latin America and the United States. La Santa Muerte does not care for anyone because love does not reign in her heart. In fact, she does not have a heart.

In conclusion to this case, what we need to do is accept Jesus Christ as our lord and savior by simply asking him to forgive us our sins as our lord and savior. The greatest decision in life is choosing Jesus Christ as your personal lord and savior.

Criminals do not lead a life of danger, crime, and the occult. Satan wants to destroy you and send you to hell, and hell will be his eternal home. Even though you lead a life of cars, boats, houses, money, sex, and alcohol, please realize that these things blind you away from the message of Jesus Christ of eternal salvation. All you have to do is ask Jesus Christ to forgive all your sins and accept him as lord and savior.

Detective Moreno knows in his heart that Jesus Christ will not let him down in times of trouble. Confronting La Santa Muerte requires a solid relationship with God Almighty, Jesus Christ, and the

Holy Spirit. Spiritual warfare leaves no survivors; it tortures, destroys, maims, and kills. Non-Christians will be pulverized by being involved with or challenging La Santa Muerte! Part of the destructive force behind the occult is men and women's involvement with it.

Psalm 18:2 says, "The Lord is my rock and my fortress and my deliverer; My God, my strength, in whom I will trust; My shield and the horn of my salvation, my stronghold." Psalm 23 says, "The Lord *is* my shepherd; I shall not want.[2] He makes me to lie down in green pastures; He leads me beside the still waters. [3] He restores my soul; He leads me in the paths of righteousness for His name's sake."

Amen.

Made in the USA
Coppell, TX
22 July 2021